BONES DON'T LIE

1430 W. Susquehanna Ave
Philadelphia, PA 19121
215-236-1760 | treehousebooks.org

BONES DON'T LIE

CURTISS T. GARDNER

WILDSIDE PRESS

For Mildred

Published by Wildside Press LLC.
www.wildsidebooks.com

ONE

The sprawling gray mills, wrapped in their eternal pall of smoke, were a lift to young Ray Locke's spirits as he first saw them from the train window in the early morning. His spirits needed a lift. It had been a long year since he last saw the Ironton plant of American-Consolidated Steel, an endless year.

Nervousness came later, after he had made the half-hour trolley ride from the city, and stood before the plant's Administration Building. Then it was only nervousness based upon the almost hopeless task confronting him.

Before he walked up the granite steps, he plucked from his vest pocket the pair of large bone dice he always carried. They had belonged to his father and he was strongly attached to them. He rattled them now in his loosely cupped hand, opened his fingers, palm flat.

Ray grimaced. "Snake eyes! Not so good."

But the dice seemed to be wrong—at first—when he was admitted to the office of the General Superintendent with no more than a ten-minute wait. He would not have been too surprised if he hadn't been admitted.

Leonard Tracy, czar of the Ironton Works, sat behind the huge, custom-built, circular desk in his elaborate private office. He was a tall, slender man of early middle age, and the double-breasted, blue pinstripe suit with knife-edge creases gave him a dapper look. Tracy was distinctly handsome. He had, in fact, such a distinguished appearance that he might have modeled for a whisky ad—except for the scar.

The scar began on Tracy's right cheek, just above the jawbone, and ran down his throat to disappear beneath his collar. It was a dull brick-red, with a brownish tinge like blood recently dried. In the process of healing, livid white scar tissue had drawn and puckered hideously, resulting in a repulsive disfigurement.

Tracy got up as Ray entered, coming around the curve of his desk with hand outstretched. "Ray Locke! Glad to see you, boy!" He waved to a deep chair upholstered in blue leather. "Sit down, Ray. How are you?"

Ray eased himself into the comfortable seat. Tracy's cordiality seemed an excellent beginning. Better than he had anticipated. But then

Tracy, he remembered, was always pleasant, the type of man who had carefully studied the art of saying, "no," without arousing resentment.

"You're looking well," Tracy went on. The usual stock phrases cloaked a crack salesman's trick of putting his own personality across by raising the other fellow's ego.

Ray Locke had taken a good look at himself in the mirror of the train washroom. He was not looking well. The dead pallor of his skin made his black eyes seem too large for his narrow, rather pointed face, as if he were recovering from a serious illness.

The bad haircut, too short, didn't help, either. And he'd noticed scattered threads of gray among the black. They hadn't been there a year ago, any of them. He was much too young for gray hairs.

"I'm fine," he said, unable to keep his eyes from the scar. "But what happened to you, Mr. Tracy?"

Leonard Tracy touched the scar with his fingertips. "Oh, this? I got myself badly burned, Ray. Shortly after you were…after you went away. I was in the hospital four months. I'll carry this reminder to my grave."

"How did it happen?"

"Around the plant." Tracy waved his hand vaguely. "Just one of those things. What brings you to Ironton, Ray?"

Ray braced himself mentally. "You're probably thinking I have an infernal crust," he said, making the plunge, "and, frankly, it has taken just about all my courage. But the fact is I need a job—badly. I thought maybe you'd give me a chance at the Ironton Works."

The General Superintendent's gray-green eyes met Ray's squarely. "When did you get out, Ray? I thought you had two more years…"

"I did. I served a full year," Ray said quietly. "They gave me a year off for good behavior. I asked for a pardon, but it was refused. I'm on probation now for a three-year period. I hope you're going to believe me when I tell you again I was absolutely innocent."

Leonard Tracy was fiddling with a sharp-pointed, steel letter opener, bending it in long, supple fingers. He hesitated, weighing his words. "I've never doubted it. Not for a moment. I told you so at the trial. Remember? Belden Locke's son didn't need to go in for petty chiseling."

Mention of his father made Ray's throat constrict. He could feel his heartbeat quicken as he awaited the other man's decision because so much more than a mere job depended upon it. His level eyes did not leave the General Superintendent's face.

Tracy said, "As long as I'm head man around these mills there's a meal ticket here for you, Ray. It's the least I can do for my old friend Belden." His eyes dropped then. An apologetic note came into his voice. "But for obvious reasons, I won't be able to put you in the Test Department. You understand, don't you?"

"Anything," Ray said quickly. "Anything at all. I expect to start at the bottom."

Tracy raised his eyes again. "That's where I'm afraid it will have to be. Otherwise, I'd be subject to criticism from our people in New York."

"I quite understand," Ray said quietly.

"We need laborers on the Open Hearth rather badly. But, of course, a man with your background and training should be able to do much better. Maybe if you tried some other plant, you could land higher up the scale to start."

"It would be the same story at any plant."

"You might use another name."

Ray could feel the hot flush creeping into his pale cheeks. The suggestion stung like a lash but he made an effort to keep resentment from creeping into his voice. "My real name is plenty good. I'm not sailing under a false flag, here or anywhere."

Tracy's probing eyes mirrored approval. "Good. Then I'll promise that what happened in the past will not stand in your way at Ironton—not while I'm here. You'll be pushed ahead as fast as I can justify it." The General Superintendent flipped a switch on the interoffice communication box on his desk top. "Mr. Harris, can you step in for a moment?"

While he waited, Ray glanced around Tracy's office. The walls were paneled in Circassian walnut. A deep, costly Chinese rug, its blue shades harmonizing beautifully with the blue leather upholstering of chairs and lounge, edged toward a stone fireplace where a neat pile of small birch logs stood ready for the touch of a match.

His eyes came back to the vast, circular desk of rare, light-colored wood and exquisite craftsmanship. Its top was clear, except for a fountain pen set with an engraved silver base, and a made-to-order desk pad of hand-tooled leather.

This office reflected the personality and orderly mind of a sixty-thousand-a-year executive. It was the kind of office Ray Locke had once hoped to earn.

Rays jaw hardened. His own atmosphere would be fumes and dust and raging heat. Instead of personally designed desk accessories, his tools would be a shovel, a slice bar, a sledge. It was up to him to bridge the chasm by his own efforts.

He'd do it, too, Ray vowed to himself. This job on the Open Hearth was his entering wedge. His real job would begin after the work shift was finished.

A bulky, monk-like man entered Tracy's office, a man with heavy jowls, a swarthy complexion and eyes incongruously light blue—hard, suspicious eyes. In contrast to the dapper Tracy, he was in shirtsleeves, his collar loosened at the neck. A half-smoked cigar was clamped in his strong white teeth.

"You've never met Mr. Quentin Harris," Tracy told Ray. "He came here after your time. Mr. Harris is Assistant General Superintendent and, therefore, second in command at Ironton."

To Harris he said, "This is Ray Locke. His father was an old friend of mine. I've promised to give Ray a job at the Open Hearth. Will you take care of the details?"

Harris shifted his cigar stump. "Locke," he said reflectively. "Ray Locke! Isn't that the name of the man who was mixed up in *The Prairie Comet* affair a year or so ago?"

"That's right. The same man."

"You're not going to have him around this plant, are you?"

Tracy said, "Twenty thousand men work in these mills, Quentin. Don't you suppose there are some thieves and maybe even a few murderers among that many?

"Possibly so. But we don't know who they are. Otherwise, they wouldn't stay here. I certainly wouldn't want to employ someone I know has a criminal record, particularly a record involving our relations with an important customer."

"You won't have to employ him," Tracy said quietly. "I'll take full responsibility."

The monk-like Assistant General Superintendent still wanted to argue the point. "How'd this man happen to come here to the general offices? Why didn't he go to the employment gate? I don't like the looks of this—"

Tracy, turning suddenly from suave salesman to decisive boss, cut him short. "I make the final decisions around here. Please do as I say. Tell Quirk I want Locke put on his payroll right away."

Harris turned on his heel. His lips were compressed. "Come with me," he ordered Ray curtly.

Harris' office adjoined Tracy's, with a connecting door cut through the walnut paneling. Like the man himself, the office differed markedly from Tracy's.

True, the walls were finished with the same expensive woodwork, but there was no built-in fireplace.

The rug on the floor was the stereotyped green seen in ten thousand business offices. And the plain, somewhat worn, walnut desk, was piled knee-deep with papers.

In another respect, the tastes and working habits of Tracy and Harris showed complete divergence. Whereas Tracy's secretary occupied a desk in the anteroom in front of his spacious quarters, Harris had his right in the room with him.

She was clattering away on her typewriter as Ray walked in at Harris' heels. Ray gave her only a casual glance, just enough to see an exceptionally pretty brunette, with glossy chestnut hair done in a short bob framing a pert, oval face.

Harris said, "Miss North, please get me Eagan at the Employment Office."

The girl dialed the phone on the edge of her desk. She spoke a moment, then flipped a switch. "All right, Mr. Harris."

"Eagan? This is Quentin Harris," the Assistant General Superintendent said into the transmitter. "I have a man here by the name of Locke. We're putting him on at the Open Hearth. I'm taking him over personally to Quirk, then I'll send him to you. You'll have to cut the red tape and take him on whether you like it or not. Mr. Tracy's orders."

Ray was conscious that the girl was regarding him curiously. Her eyes were soft and brown behind the plain lenses of reading glasses. The glasses were set in a frame of red-tinted plastic which matched exactly the shade of lipstick she wore and the vermilion of her sheer, silk blouse.

Harris got to his feet. "Let's go," he said brusquely. His voice softened as he told the girl, "I'll be back shortly, Jackie."

Ray followed him from the office building and through a gate in the high fence surrounding the plant. A guard in a blue uniform, with the words *Iron and Steel Police* on his visored cap, saluted respectfully.

"Give this man a visitor's badge," Harris ordered. "I'll be responsible for him." To Ray, as they moved on, he added, "After you've got your number at the Employment Office you can turn in the temporary badge on your way out."

The tall stacks of blast furnaces, with their batteries of stoves, towered to the right of them as Harris led the way across a maze of narrow-gauge tracks toward long, gray buildings a quarter of a mile away. Ray could hear the rumble of skips carrying loads of ore, coke and limestone up inclines to the loading bells. Signal whistles shrilled in orderly confusion.

Ray knew the route they were taking, knew it almost as well as Harris.

"I don't need to take any more of your time," he suggested to the big man at his side. "I can find my own way to the Open Hearth. I've been there often."

"I know that," Harris retorted. "You've been there too often." His words were an accusation. "You'd never go there again if I had my way."

Angry words were on Ray's lips. He bit them back. "Why not give me a break?" be asked. "You don't know the whole story. What good does it do to kick a fellow when he's down?"

"It's your own fault you're down," Harris said.

"I wasn't any more responsible for that faulty axle than you were," Ray said stoutly.

"Who was?"

"I don't know." It was on the tip of his tongue to add, "That's what I'm going to find out," but be didn't say it.

Quirk, Superintendent of the Open Hearth, was a little Irishman with a wide, good-humored mouth and a wrinkle of crow's-feet around his bright, restless eyes. He wore a pair of stained corduroy pants and a flannel shirt open at the neck.

"Here's a new man for you," Harris told him shortly. "Tracy wants him to start right away."

"New man?" There was recognition in Quirk's sharp eyes, and a suggestion of scorn in the way his lips curled at the corners. "Nothing new about Locke to me. I know him from way back." He turned to Harris belligerently. "What's the idea? You putting Locke here to show me how to make steel?"

"*I'm* not putting him here." Harris was emphatic. "Ask Mr. Tracy the idea. And this man is not working *with* you, he's working *for* you—anywhere you can use him."

"Now ain't that just fine!" Quirk's eyes stabbed swiftly at Ray. "Locke used to tell me when he didn't like my steel. Now I'll tell him a thing or two."

Ray said, "Okay, Mike Quirk. You dish it out. I can take it."

Quirk said, "I need men. I'm short-handed. You'll be on the four-to-midnight shift." He grinned suddenly. "We'll let you dip tests for the hoys at the lab. You can start tonight."

Locke grinned back at the little Super. "Okay. I'm pretty good at that."

It was still before eleven when Ray finished the routine at the Employment Office. He'd been thumped by the company doctor, had filled out pages of personal data. In spite of Tracy's sponsorship, and the fact that he was hired regardless, the regular procedure had to be followed.

Out in the sunshine again, Ray stopped to consider. His peculiar sleeping habits would be something of a problem now. Over the years he had reached the conclusion that people spent too much of their lives in bed. Scientists had proved that from two to four hours' sleep was ample, provided short naps were taken during the day whenever the body showed any signs of fatigue. The results, of course, were most gratifying—at least six extra hours added to the day. What a lot of constructive things people could do with those six additional hours!

Ray had followed this program assiduously during his earlier years at Ironton, much to the amusement of the other plant workers who had grown accustomed to seeing him snatch forty winks in some dark, deserted corner at various times during the day. He couldn't hope to resume this routine immediately, of course, and, anyway, he'd been out of practice for a year. He could get back by easy stages.

There had been six dollars in his pocket when he reached Ironton. Two of them he had already put out as a deposit on a barren room in a crummy, frame rooming house, half a mile from the main gate into Ironton. Three more went now for a pair of work pants and a blue denim shirt.

He took a half-hour nap on the hard bed in his new, shabby living quarters, awaking completely refreshed. He put on his work clothes and went again to the mills.

It was still nearly three hours before he was due on shift at the Open Hearth. On his way through tire noisy, clanging plant, Ray remembered how it had been a year ago.

He'd been a man with a future, then, a man groomed from early boyhood for big things. When he visited the Ironton Works of American-Consolidated Steel, he stayed in a good room at the best hotel in town. He came out to the plant in a taxi, with a rosebud in his lapel. As a representative of the Transcontinental Line, one of the steel company's biggest customers, he was treated with deference by all the plant men.

Ray shrugged. That was ancient history. He did not doubt his reception now would be vastly different.

TWO

The Test Department at Ironton occupied in entirety a small, two-story building in almost the geodetic center of the four-mile plant. The ground floor of the aged, brick structure was filled with physical testing equipment. There were machines for determining tensile strength, for making bending, torsion and drop tests and all the supplemental devices for accurate testing of steel, including a Shore scleroscope and a machine for obtaining Brinell hardness.

Beyond the big room with the apparatus was the small private office of the Engineer of Tests, and a somewhat larger office containing three desks for clerical help. The wall space in the larger office was jammed with filing cabinets of old test records.

The upstairs of the building was devoted exclusively to a large, completely equipped, chemical laboratory.

Ray walked in through an outer room edged with bins where broken test specimens awaited return to the scrap pile and ultimately the furnaces. In the middle of the floor stood a heavy, wooden table, scarred like a butchers chopping block.

At the table a man with shirtsleeves rolled to the elbows and a pipe clenched in his teeth was busy with a ball-peen hammer and a box of steel dies putting numbers on small iron blocks. At first glance the man had a startling resemblance to an exhumed corpse.

Skeleton thinness was not responsible for the impression. The man was average-sized and not at all emaciated. It was the bony structure of his head which first caught the eye, that and the earthy brownness of his coloring.

The head was large at the top with very prominent cheekbones over which the skin drew tightly. It tapered to a weak receding chin. The taut skin and sunken cheeks made the configuration of the entire skull strikingly evident.

The earthy color started with the skin, which was a muddy hue vastly different from the healthy bronze which comes from clean outdoor living. The man's hair was brown, too, and commencing to thin. His small mustache was such a light shade of brown as to be almost invisible. Even the frayed and shabby business suit he wore had faded from its original shade of brown to a claylike hue.

He glanced up casually as Ray entered, looked back at his work, then suddenly dropped the hammer as delayed recognition reached his brain.

"Am I seeing ghosts, or is it really Ray Locke?"

He took the pipe from his mouth and advanced with hand extended. His eyes behind rimless glasses were friendly.

"In the flesh!" Ray said. "Just thought I'd come in and say hello, Ben, to you and all the laboratory folks. Didn't want to shock you too much if you happened to bump into me around the plant."

Benjamin Gaylord was sizing up Ray's coarse pants and denim shirt. "Don't tell me you're working at Ironton? Say, that's splendid! It is a surprise because…well, I thought…"

He stopped and an expression of embarrassment spread over his death's head features.

"Yeah. I know." Ray let it go at that. "Are all the old gang still around?"

"Some of them. Ashley is still Engineer of Tests. And Clara Dunne is Chief Chemist. Walter Keene is still in the chemical lab. You remember Walter, don't you?

Ray nodded.

"Most of the others you knew have left. A lot of them were in the service." Gaylord hesitated, then added, "I'm Chief Inspector, now. Maybe you knew that?"

Ray wondered if Gaylord expected congratulations on his promotion. He didn't begrudge the man advancement. Someone had to fill Glenn Cannon's old job.

But Ray couldn't bring himself to utter the customary platitudes. Not when he knew that death and heartbreak and two shattered careers, his own and Cannon's, had been responsible for Gaylord's step up the ladder.

"So I heard!" he said quietly. "I suppose it's all right for me to go upstairs?"

Gaylord said, "Sure. They'll be glad to see you." He jerked his head toward the hammer and the stamps. "I've got to get these specimens ready. I'll be seeing you later."

Christopher Ashley was not in his own office. Ray found him on the second floor, in the tiny cubicle belonging to the Chief Chemist, near the head of the stairs. The Engineer of Tests was looking through a stack of reports on the Chief Chemist's desk. His small, neat, pointed beard and absent-minded, brown eyes gave him the appearance of a college professor.

"We've got to take care of those carbon-vanadium forgings for the New Haven, today," Ashley began, as he heard Ray's feet on the stairs and swiveled in his chair. "Let's make sure…"

He broke off when he saw Ray. That he recognized him was evident. His mild, scholarly face assumed a grim expression. "Thought I was talking to Gaylord. What are *you* doing around here, Locke?"

Ray ignored the coolness. He smiled. "I'm working over at the Open Hearth. Dropped in to see if I'd been entirely forgotten."

"How could any of us forget you?" Ashley asked pointedly. He swiveled to the papers again, his back to Ray.

Ray couldn't blame Ashley for the lack of cordiality. In Ashley's book, Ray was a man convicted of petty chicanery that had cost human lives—many lives. As responsible head of the Test Department, Ashley had come in for plenty of criticism himself.

For a moment Ray stood looking at the big man's broad back and stooped shoulders. He wished he could he sure in his own mind about Ashley. On the surface it seemed impossible that such a studious man, one apparently devoted whole-heartedly to technical metallurgical problems, could be mixed up in the kind of skullduggery which had made twisted wreckage of *The Prairie Comet.* On the other hand, it would he strange if such things could go on in the department without knowledge of the boss.

A woman was standing with her back to Ray as he walked into the chemical laboratory. She was wearing a white twill laboratory coat which concealed her stocky figure and clothing, but he recognized Clara Dunne from the odd, white streak in her blond hair at the nape of the neck. They used to kid Clara about that streak, Ray remembered. The white hairs, she always stoutly insisted, were a birthmark.

"When you've finished the titration," Clara was calling to someone behind a laboratory bench that cut off Ray's range of vision, "add one cc of 0.1 per cent $K_3Fe(CN)_6$ solution. Be very careful when you put in the ferrous sulphate. As soon as the green color appears, let me know and I'll show you what to do next."

Ray stepped through the door. "Hello, Clara," he said.

She turned. She wasn't exactly a girl. Ray had wondered about Clara Dunne's real age. She was one of those women who retain their good looks until beyond middle age, though Clara certainly had a long way to go yet before she reached her halfway milepost.

Ten years ago she must have been a real beauty. Her features were still regular and well-formed. But there was a trifle too much fleshiness now. It showed in her cheeks and in the curve of her throat. It would have been quite noticeable in her still strong, muscular figure if she had not been wearing the loose laboratory coat. As someone had once irreverently remarked, Clara Dunne was built like a wrestler.

"Hello, Mr. Locke," she said.

Just like that. No surprise, no questions such as the others had asked. She might have seen him in the laboratory only last week, or yesterday.

That was typical of Clara, Ray reflected. Her calm, cool efficiency was what had made her head of the Ironton chemical laboratory a long time ago, with men twice her age working under her direction.

"You're looking the same as ever, Clara," he began. "I see…"

A small, runty man came around the end of the nearest laboratory bench. He fastened his sharp, beady eyes on Ray.

"Well, well, well!" he remarked unpleasantly. "If it isn't the prodigal son! Who turned *you* loose on an unsuspecting community? I thought you were safely out of the way for a long time yet."

Ray had never cared much for Walter Keene. In fact he had never come much in contact with the laboratory assistant. Keene was simply one of the people in the background. Perhaps, Ray reminded himself, it might be one of those unimportant background people who had played a major part in the tragedy of the defective axle. That's what he had come back to Ironton to find out.

He gave no sign of the resentment Keene's biting remarks had caused. He forced a smile.

"I'm back," he said evenly, "but not exactly like the prodigal son. No one has bothered to kill the fatted calf for me."

"Why should they?" Keene asked. Then, "Is Glenn Cannon out of jail, too?"

Ray said, "I haven't seen Glenn." He was fighting an overwhelming desire to smash Walter Keene in the mouth.

"No, I guess you wouldn't have seen him at that. Not where you've been."

Ray decided to ignore the man. His glance traveled the big room with its glass shelves loaded with reagent bottles, its complicated glassware and tubing, and its pale, glowing Bunsen flames.

"Lots of new faces," he remarked to Clara. "Mostly girls, I see."

There had been no women employees in the lab except Clara a year ago.

"We lost a lot of people during the war," she said. "Lucky to have kept a few 4-Fs like Walter."

The reminder irritated Keene. He took it out on Ray.

"I understand the Army didn't take convicts, either," he said bitterly. "What classification did the draft board give you, Locke?"

Rays fist clenched; he took an involuntary step forward.

"Too much is enough," he told Keene icily. "If you're trying to start something, squirt, you've done it."

Clara Dunne stepped between the two men. "Get back to your titration, Walter," she ordered.

Keene turned on his heel. A mocking grin twisted his thin, wrinkled face. "Once upon a time," he said loudly as he walked toward his bench at the rear of the laboratory, "there was a big gun around this plant, named Cannon. But Cannon was finally fired. There was a lot of noise and quite a bad smell, too, but no one got hurt except Cannon, who was busted, and a kid inspector who wasn't dry yet behind the ears."

Ray Locke's face was red with fury. His black eyes glowed menacingly.

"I'll split your head open," he threatened.

Clara's hand on his arm restrained his forward move. "You'd better go, now," she told him. Her voice was calm, as always. "I won't have any rough stuff around my laboratory."

As he went down the stairs, Ray could hear her reproving Walter Keene. "You've been asking for trouble lately. If you don't watch yourself, you're going to find some."

And he heard Keene's insolent, jarring laugh.

Ray set off through the plant, walking aimlessly, not going anywhere, but simply trying to relieve the upset of his mind by physical exercise.

He hadn't expected excessive cordiality from all his former acquaintances inside the Ironton Works. Chris Ashley's indifference or Quirk's slight malicious riding was about as anticipated. But sheer vindictiveness such as Walter Keene had shown was beyond the bounds of reason.

To the left of the Test Department building was the blank side wall of the forge shop. Ray could feel the earth shake beneath his feet under the impact of the sixteen-thousand-pound steam hammers housed in the structure.

He turned in the other direction, past the vast, five-acre machine shop, where all kinds of steel products from six-inch test specimens to giant coast defense guns were being shaped and finished.

He went past the machine shop to the more thickly clustered mill buildings, and beyond, to the open stretch pocked with cinder dumps and piles of blooms. He crossed that, wandering past coal trestles and the towers which carried power wires, toward the docks and ore piles to the left of the blast furnaces.

Was this an impossible task he had set himself? Ray wondered. So many people might have had a hand in the crookedness for which he had served time in the Big House. He remembered Tracy's remark that upward of twenty thousand persons were employed in this, one of the largest steel mills in all America. The fact that a whole year had elapsed since the calamity in question was, to Ray, like the further handicap of being obliged to wear boxing gloves during his haystack needle hunt.

Ray's chin came up. His determination must be slight indeed if he could be discouraged at the very start by insults from a laboratory assistant he hardly knew. Too much depended upon his success for him to waver. He was fighting for his father's dreams, for his own good name, and the regard of his fellow men.

The task could not be quite so formidable as he pictured it. Whoever in the vast plant might have been involved in the scandal, reason dictated it could not have been accomplished without the active knowledge and assistance of someone in the Test Department.

That narrowed the field to a mere handful of people. Not only an employee of the Test Department, but someone in a position of responsibility must be involved.

He ticked them off mentally. Ashley? He had already considered the Engineer of Tests. In his opinion Ashley was a thoroughly honest man.

Clara Dunne? From what sleepless nights had told him during his year in the penitentiary, the type of conniving involved would have made necessary the falsification of physical as well as chemical tests. Clara had nothing to do with the physical end of the department.

The same applied to Clara's assistants, like Walter Keene. The chemists would have had even less opportunity than Clara to plan and execute the whole affair. Still, it *might* have been done.

By the same reasoning, the plant's Chief Inspector had no hand in chemical tests. Glenn Cannon had been Chief Inspector at the time of the disaster. Cannon, like himself, had said he was framed.

Briefly he considered Ben Gaylord. Gaylord's position in the physical laboratory, at that time, had been similar to Keene's in the chemical—a principal assistant. But he might have had better opportunity than Keene for engineering a complete falsification of the tests.

Ray sighed. He had come to the edge of the coal docks and stood looking across the narrow inlet which marked the end of the plant at this side. The choppy water with its swift, treacherous current reminded him of Hell Gate in New York.

Out on the water, a barge bringing fresh heaps of coal for the maws of the insatiable furnaces, maneuvered toward its berth at the dock. Beyond the barge, at the far side of the channel, the light structural cobwebs of an electric power substation were silhouetted against the sky beside the rusty stacks of obsolete blast furnaces, once operated by the Ironton Works, but now long since abandoned.

Ray turned. He'd wandered nearly two miles through the long plant. He should get back somewhere near the Open Hearth.

He avoided the test laboratory on his return trip and took a route past the splice-bar mill. The smell of hot metal as it came from the shears and turned slowly on the big wheel through an oil quenching bath was pungent in his nostrils. Ray remembered with a pang how in better days he had inspected splice-bars by the carload for the railroad.

He lingered a moment in the looping mill, watching the leather-gloved men in front of the rolls catch fiery serpents of round bar steel with tongs, whirling the glowing loops around their heads and inserting the end into the other level of the rolls.

With a little shudder he remembered the time he had seen a green workman miss his aim with the end of the bar. How the escaped loop, contracting around the man, had burned him in half with the ease of a hot knife cutting butter.

Ray was glad Leonard Tracy had not put him to work in the looping mill, one of the most dangerous jobs in a dangerous industry.

From the end of the plate mill, Ray could see the Pen Hearth building. He consulted his watch. Three-fifteen. He could take his half-hour nap before reporting to work. It wasn't quite time for sleeping, but he'd already decided that his usual schedule must be modified in part. This was a good chance to experiment.

The reheating furnaces were at the other end of the long mill structure. Where Ray stood, finished plates were piled in great stacks, hundreds of tons in weight. Ray picked a pile against the side of the corrugated iron wall. A hard bed, but it was not the first time he'd snatched a nap in some equally unlikely place.

He was settling himself on the topmost plate, when a peculiar splotch attracted his attention. He rubbed the tips of his fingers over the hard steel surface tentatively. It was slightly oily. He got to his feet again to take a better look.

The oily spot was almost nine feet long, wider at both ends than in the middle, like a distorted hourglass. In the center of the splotch was a four-inch dusting of whitish powder.

Ray knew then what had caused the mark. He'd seen similar things in the days when he used to inspect plates for "pits" and "snakes" and other defects.

Some workman had eaten lunch while sitting on this plate. There had been a chicken leg in the lunch box and the man had left the meatless bone on the plate. Other plates had been piled on top. Under such terrific pressure, grease from the bone had been squeezed out to form a grease spot in the exact shape of a monstrous chicken bone.

Ray went to sleep almost instantly. But, contrary to usual habit, his sleep was neither complete nor restful. Perhaps this was because his previous nap was only four hours past instead of the usual six. Or maybe this excitement of seeing old familiar sights and faces was responsible, making him live again unpleasant memories.

It was a dream, yet the actual record of what he had lived in the past. The clank and grind of the plate rolls, five hundred feet from him in the mill, became the roar of *The Prairie Comet*, westward bound with Ray Locke asleep in Bedroom B. Whistle blasts from the boss rollers platform, signaling that the rolling of a certain size plate had been completed, became the *Comet's* locomotive, shrilling for a crossing.

His nightmare terror, building to a known and heart-chilling climax, was synchronized exactly with the clang of plates deposited from a traveling crane upon a pile fifty feet distant.

That crash, to Ray Locke, was satanic din from the stricken *Comet*. He heard again the rending of steel cars, the shriek of escaping steam, the swift-rising screams of the mangled and dying. It was as if a giant's fist had hammered down, to sweep the train from its rails into a mass of twisted wreckage.

There was a hoarse cry in Ray's throat as he suddenly bolted upright from the hard plates. He was still half asleep, half awake. Vivid in his mind, as if he were seeing it again, was his father's dead face when Belden Locke's body was cut with an acetylene torch from the tangle of steel which had been Bedroom A.

There was sweat on Ray's forehead. He had wished more than once that he and not his father had been the occupant of the bedroom nearer the end of the telescoped car. For after three weeks in the hospital, Ray had emerged to find responsibility for the wreck laid squarely on his own doorstep.

One of the axles on the *Comet's* locomotive had snapped, falling to the track, throwing the train off the rails and across the right of way squarely into the path of an eastbound express which had completed the disaster by plowing into the derailed Pullmans three minutes later.

The railroad had been prompt to disclaim negligence. The broken axle was one of a shipment from the Ironton Works of American-Consolidated Steel. It had been duly inspected by a supposedly competent railroad inspector—Ray Locke.

After the damage had been done, metallurgical tests showed that the axle had been dangerously defective when put into service. For use as locomotive axles, the steel, deficient in vanadium, high in both sulphur and phosphorus content, was virtually rotten. Tension tests fell twenty thousand pounds per square inch below the point required by railroad specifications.

Negligence on the part of the inspector was clearly indicated. Ordinarily, Ray would have lost his job with the railroad, suffered a black mark against his reputation, and that would have been all. As it happened, two old wooden sleepers filled with troops had been smashed to match-wood in the wreck. Seventy-two soldiers were dead and nearly as many civilians. The wreck had immediate political repercussions. And a short time later, while Ray was still in the hospital, letters had been discovered among Glenn Cannon's papers by government investigators: letters in which Glenn Cannon, as the steel company's Chief Inspector, allegedly agreed to pay Ray for the acceptance of steel known to fall far short of requirements.

After that, the case took on a criminal aspect. Ray was convicted on three counts: of accepting a bribe, of willful neglect of duty, and of involuntary manslaughter. His sentences, to run concurrently, had been three to five years.

Deep grooves were cut into Rays forehead as he got up and stalked out of the plate mill. He remembered the tests on that particular shipment of axles as clearly as if he had just made them. They should have been clear in his mind; he'd had a year to think about them.

The chemical analysis had been quite okay at the time. And the tension test had developed a yield point at seventy thousand pounds per square inch and a tensile strength of one hundred and ten thousand.

The minimum called for in the specifications had been fifty-eight thousand and ninety thousand respectively.

The discrepancy was baffling to Ray. Many were the nights he had spent lying sleeplessly in his cell conjuring up, and then rejecting, one explanation after another. His whole plan of life, now that he was on parole, centered upon discovering the method of falsifying tests, and in so doing, exposing the criminal who had blasted his career.

Ray quickened his steps to reach the entrance of the Open Hearth. It was a place of vast gloom and blinding brilliance, direct from the pages of Dante; a place of cinders, of showering golden sparks and of grinding labor, with Satan's assistants dressed in grimy overalls.

Flaming gases hissed through tortuous underground chambers. Mechanical monsters clanged their way to add their ingredients to a Devil's brew of white hot metal. Rivers of liquid steel and glowing slag burst forth periodically in a man-made, man-controlled Inferno.

This was the Open Hearth, not so spectacular as the Bessemer with its thirty-foot plumes of volcanic flame, but spectacular nonetheless, and a more practical, modern and proven method of making steel. Ray Locke had always liked the Open Hearth.

A green man would have been started shoveling dolomite—raw dolomite and burnt dolomite—or cleaning up slag splashes, cinders and other debris around the furnaces. He'd have been given some job where he probably would not be killed his first day on the job.

Knowing Ray's familiarity with the steel-making technique, Quirk had him place the spout for a furnace about to be tapped, dig the mud and fireclay stopper from the furnace tap-hole, and dip test specimens of molten metal from the glowing bath with a small hand ladle. The duties were actually those of a second helper.

It was gratifying to Ray how quickly he recalled skills not used for a long time; how, even before the end of that first shift, he was stepping nonchalantly across the first thin trickle of liquid metal in the spout as it started to flow down into the giant ladle below the furnace platform. He could still tell accurately from the star-shaped sparks o the initial test specimen, broken and held against an emery wheel, that the melt was too high in carbon and needed addition of feed ore before the heat should be tapped.

Not that his opinion was asked or that he volunteered it. Control of the furnaces rested with the first helper and the melter, and with the little, bright-eyed Quirk, who usually managed to be on the platform behind every furnace at tapping time. The wiry, Irish Super seemed always on the job. Ray wondered if, like himself, Quirk had discovered the scientific method of getting along with very little sleep.

Ray kept his mouth shut and did as he was told. Quirk tried to ride him a bit at first, but when he saw that Ray took what he dished out with no anger or sullenness, he soon let his new helper alone.

There was nothing wrong with Quirk, Ray decided. In spite of what the man had said to Harris, Rays contact with the actual manufacture of steel at Ironton had been very slight. There was no real reason the Open Hearth Superintendent should have it in for him, other than the feeling, understandable in any supervisory employee at Ironton, that Ray had smirched the plant's good name.

It was nearly midnight and Ray was down on the pouring floor, or cinder-pit, of the plant, walking below the line of furnaces on his way to Number Eight. Number Three had been tapped. The melter had ordered him to help make bottom on Number Eight.

He was under the platform of Number Five, plodding along with his head down, thinking about what he intended to do when he got off shift, when suddenly something whizzed past his head, so close he could feel a breeze from its passing. It landed with a heavy thump in the dirt near his feet.

He ducked involuntarily, although the danger was already past. Then he looked to see what had missed him. It was a lump of jagged, scabby steel, evidently a splash broken from some ingot during cooling.

The fragment must have weighed every ounce of twenty pounds. Had it struck Ray on the head, he would have been lucky to escape with a simple fracture. More likely his skull would have been caved in.

Ray's eyes turned quickly upward. The overhang of the furnace platform was some twenty feet above the cinder-pit floor. No one was on the platform, but he did get a fleeting glimpse of something disappearing through the alley to the charging floor between Number Five and Six furnaces.

He wasn't even sure he had seen a man, just a glimpse of something blue. Then it was gone. It might have been a pair of clean blue overalls, but Ray's impression was of a brighter blue than overalls.

Juggling the steel lump in his hand, he stood staring up. Maybe there had been nothing blue on the platform after all. Maybe it had just been imagination. But the heavy, jagged fragment was not imagination.

How, he wondered, had it fallen? Someone might have kicked it from the platform; someone not thinking of the danger to a man passing below. It is always a bad matter not to think, particularly in a spot as hazardous as the Open Hearth.

Could the steel have been dislodged from higher up by vibration from the giant traveling crane which had just passed? That seemed a far-fetched theory. Cooling ingots do not cast off fragments which cling to the roof trusses fully seventy feet above.

Neither explanation seemed credible to Ray. There was a third one: that someone had deliberately dropped or thrown the steel with the express purpose of hitting him, and, after throwing it and observing the near miss, had ducked from sight onto the charging floor.

A flight of iron-treaded stairs led up to the furnaces. Ray went up them fast.

The door of Number Five furnace was open; a man in blue glasses stood peering at the seething metal within. Hunkies were shoveling dolomite into a buggy on the narrow gauge tracks. Farther along the charging floor a burly man in the uniform of the *Iron and Steel Police* stood watching the hunkies.

No one else was in sight.

THREE

Ray went off shift at midnight. The vast Ironton Works, roaring along full blast, night as well as daytime, was a place of dazzling lights and deep black shadows. But the light on the second floor of the testing laboratory was dim. Only one sleepy chemist should be on duty to give carbon content on test samples submitted before the tapping of an open hearth furnace, or the teeming of a converter blow.

To spend a night alone in the deserted laboratory would be a tiresome vigil for the average man, Ray knew. Tests were only required at intervals, often hours apart. Five minutes' work and they were done. In between, Ray figured, the chemist on duty would be dozing in a corner, drawing pay mainly for his broken night's rest.

The trick, then, was simply to avoid any loud racket which might alarm the chemist. Keeping in the shadows, Ray approached the old brick building. He eased the door open cautiously, careful to avoid a squeaking hinge.

Halfway across the outer room he stopped dead in his tracks. A light had switched on downstairs near Ashley's office.

Ray melted into the gloom beside the bins with their broken test pieces. His feet struck something soft and yielding. Instantly the hush of the quiet building was broken by an earsplitting uproar like the scream of a banshee, and something small and white streaked for the stairway, emitting hair-raising yowls as it fled.

It was Oscar, the laboratory cat.

Ray hesitated. With the night man roaming around downstairs and the squalling cat at large, another hour's wait might be advisable, to let things quiet down again.

Halfway back to the door Ray's plans received their third setback. The electric bulbs in the outer room went on.

Ray turned. The glib story he had ready on the tip of his tongue for the night chemist died on his lips. The person staring at him from the door of the physical lab was a girl—a girl in a red silk blouse, a girl with a pert oval face framed in glossy chestnut hair. Quentin Harris' secretary, Jackie North!

"You!" she exclaimed sharply. Her brown eyes were large with fright and the color had drained from her cheeks.

There was a sound from the rooms at the other end of the test lab, like file drawers being pushed quickly shut. A man's face was framed suddenly in the lighted doorway beyond the row of tall, black testing machines.

The face belonged to a big, powerfully built man, and it wore a perfectly dead-pan expression like a movie gangster. Yet, even in the fleeting glimpse Ray caught as the man turned swiftly, the features twitched convulsively, contorting the man's face into a hideous, leering grimace.

Many times in the past, Ray had seen a similar nervous spasm twist that same face. There could be no mistaking it, even though he had believed the man afflicted with the facial tic to be many miles away from Ironton.

He leaped forward, pushing Jackie North out of his way. "Cannon!" he called. "Glenn Cannon!"

In the rear a door with a squeaky hinge opened and shut again quickly. When Ray reached the short corridor beside Christopher Ashley's private office, the man was gone.

He pulled the door open and looked out. Windows of the vast machine shop, a ghastly shade of blue from scores of mercury arc lights, were at his right. To the left, its earth-shaking hammers stilled for the night, the forge shop lifted its blank side wall. Of Glenn Cannon there was not the slightest trace.

Jackie North had come back from the outer room and was standing near the scale arm of the big Norton testing machine. Even in the excitement and surprise of seeing Cannon, Ray found himself thinking of the girl's beauty rather than the upset to his own plans.

He hadn't really appreciated her back in the executive offices. But here in the laboratory, at two in the morning, she gave him a queer stimulation. A stimulation half mental, half physical. He would like, he thought, to…

Abruptly he jerked himself back to sanity. What was the matter with him? he wondered. It must be the old saying about sap rising swiftly in the young tree in early springtime.

"And I'm the sap!" he said, unconscious that he had spoken aloud.

Jackie North was looking at him queerly. "I didn't think you knew it," she said quite seriously.

Ray said, "I didn't know Glenn Cannon was back at Ironton."

"He isn't back. Tracy practically threw Glenn out of his office."

A surprising note of bitterness had crept into her tone. "It isn't everyone who has the effect on Tracy that you have."

Ray was astonished. "Effect? Why did Tracy throw Cannon out?"

"Don't ask me." Jackie had recovered her poise in full. "Cannon came in just as you did. He wanted a job. *He* didn't get it. It doesn't seem fair."

"What's Glenn Cannon to you?" Ray asked sharply.

"Nothing."

"How did he get inside the plant? And what're you doing here with him?"

"I don't know anything about Cannon," Jackie retorted. "And though it's none of your business, Mr. Harris asked me to come here. He happens to be my boss."

"An office girl? At this hour of the night?"

"The pot calling the kettle black," she said, smiling acidly. "You're here, too."

"I work the night shift," he informed her curtly, listening to the footsteps coming down the stairs.

The runty, sharp-featured Walter Keene appeared. Just at his back was Clara Dunne. She was not wearing her laboratory coat.

Keene's mouth twisted in an unpleasant smile. "Miss Dunne, we'd better put new locks on all the doors while Mr. Locke is anywhere within ten miles of the lab. He might try to have more rotten steel built into trains."

Ray's jaws clamped tight. "I warned you this afternoon, Keene. Keep on with that kind of talk and I'm going to meet you outside the plant one of these days and take you apart."

Clara Dunne said, "What have you people been doing to poor Oscar? He came upstairs as if he'd been shot out of a gun. He's hiding under one of the reagent shelves and won't come out."

"It was dark when I walked in," Ray told her, trying to match her own quiet tone. "I stepped on his tail, I'm afraid. I didn't expect to find you here tonight."

"And I certainly didn't expect to see you," she countered. "You must be up to your old tricks. I remember how you used to sleep around in odd corners and then be up all hours of the night."

"I'm on nights at the Open Hearth now," he explained, neglecting to add that his shift had ended more than an hour before. "I was just coming in to check on the last melt in Number Three furnace."

"There aren't any hours on *this* job anymore," Clara complained. "If there were more than twenty-four hours in a day, I'd work that much longer." She turned to Keene. "Walter, you get the report on the test he wants."

Ray started to follow Keene up the stairs, but she stopped him. "I think maybe you'd better let him bring it down. I don't want to be picking up pieces from the floor of my laboratory."

When Keene returned a few moments later, Ray left. As he passed the lighted windows of the machine shop, he saw Ben Gaylord. The Chief Inspector was in a huddle near a lathe with two other men. One was a thin, consumptive-looking machinist in a greasy work cap. The other was a big, burly giant with a thick neck and unshaven cheeks grimed with soot. The three were carefully examining a test specimen which the machinist had just removed from his lathe.

Ray Locke grinned mirthlessly to himself. At two o'clock in the morning the place was swarming with people. Almost everyone connected with the Test Department, except Ashley himself, was not more than a stone's throw away. A fine night he had chosen for snooping around the test laboratory.

Words, floating out through the open window, stopped him as he was about to pass along.

"This looks okay!" the Chief Inspector was saying as he handed the test piece back to the machinist.

"How about them Gulf Southeastern axles?" the huge man inquired anxiously.

The word "axles" halted Ray and caused him to listen intently from his vantage point outside.

"We'll save the inspector some time on that job, too," Gaylord declared. "You'd better make the hollow borings on those axles tomorrow, Al." And as he turned away, he added to the machinist, "We'll send you some cores from heat 557831 in the morning, Pete."

Locke stood rooted to the spot, immobilized by the excitement burning through him. For Gaylord's words, innocent enough in themselves, provided the first gleam of light on the question that had caused Ray so many sleepless hours. He felt certain now, as certain as one could of a theory, as yet untested, that he had the key piece to the puzzle.

* * * *

Like hot saws in the rail mill, the loud snores of other men who had worked the night shift ripped through the flimsy walls of the rooming house. But Ray did not sleep. With an extension cord and a dime-store socket, he rigged the one naked electric bulb from its ceiling cord, making it into a reading light over the sagging Morris chair beside the room's one and only window.

The window admitted air conditioned with odors of garbage, gas leaks and stale beer from the taproom next door. Liberally mingled was the all-pervading Ironton atmosphere of smoke fumes from mills and furnaces.

At nine in the morning Ray was turning the pages of his well-thumbed Carnegie Steel handbook, *The Making, Shaping and Treatment of Steel.* So little daylight filtered through his back window that he still had the bulb burning. He reached up to switch it off. The chemical reactions inside a blast furnace were beginning to grow wearisome. A rest was in order.

Just at that moment the door was flung open without warning. A man in the uniform of the company police strode unceremoniously into the room, a huge, burly man whose protruding jaw and cauliflower ear made him look like an ex-prize fighter.

Ray suddenly recalled the policeman he had seen on the platform behind Number Five furnace the night before. This looked like the same man.

"So I found you!" the cop exclaimed. His tone implied that this fact was a major surprise.

"Not very difficult," Ray observed, "since I put my address on the employment form in two places." He surveyed the thick-set man without enthusiasm. "I didn't hear you knock."

The cop flexed a huge, hairy hand suggestively. "You'll hear me knock! With my fist against your noggin if you get smart!"

Ray tossed the book onto his bed. "What gives me the unexpected pleasure of this delightful visit?"

His sarcasm was entirely lost on the big bruiser. "The pleasure is all mine, bud," the man said. "I thought sure you'd have scrammed out of here quick, before we nabbed you. Guess you ain't quite bright."

Ray was puzzled. "If you'll tell me what this is all about…"

"You know! Get your hat, fellow. You and me are goin' over to the test lab."

"The test lab," Ray parroted. "Why…"

"Cut out the gab," the big cop ordered. "Do you come along quiet or do I give you a workout first?" Ray's heart sank. His fingers reached for his dice. They showed a pair of sixes.

"Boxcars," he said.

"Just a box," the cop remarked. "One plain, pine box! You've crapped out of the game right now."

It wasn't reassuring.

Ray went with the man without further argument. There wasn't anything else he could do. He made another attempt to find out what was behind it all, but the cop refused to talk. His whole attitude was tough and strangely ominous.

When he saw the other cops milling around the Test Department building Ray began to realize that something serious was involved. Not only company cops were outside the old brick structure but others—men from the regular city police.

Upstairs in the chemical laboratory were more cops and men in business suits wearing square-toed shoes and derby hats, men on whose faces the label '*plainclothes detective*' was easy to read.

All the Test Department people were there, too. Not only Ashley and Gaylord and Clara Dunne, but, crowding around eagerly, excited small fry, the chemists and men who ran the apparatus in the physical lab.

Even the plant big shots, Tracy and Harris, were there, standing somewhat apart from the others in the open space between the door of the chemical laboratory and the first row of laboratory benches. With them was a large, muscular-appearing man, partially bald and wearing a scrubby, black mustache.

Ray had seen this man before. He remembered how an awestricken employee of the Ironton Works had once pointed him out as U. G. Flint, a representative of the steel combine's governing hierarchy in New York and a man to whom even Tracy must defer.

"I see you've got him, Bixler." Harris was speaking to the bruiser who had brought Ray from the rooming house. The monk-like Assistant General Superintendent's pale blue eyes stabbed at Ray accusingly.

The company cop grinned, exposing plentiful gold caps among his tobacco-stained teeth. "I got him, sir," he said proudly. "'Windpipe' Bixler always gets his man.

The way he said it gave the impression of a Canadian Mountie closing in on his quarry after endless days on the long trail and a furious hand-to-hand struggle.

Harris turned to LI. G. Flint. "I feel sure this is the guilty party, General. He's an ex-convict with a shameful record. It's a wonder to me we found him at all. He's had time to get a hundred miles away."

Bixler said, "He was up an' dressed, gettin' ready to scram when I nabbed him."

Swift anger burned through Ray. "It happens I was in my room quietly reading when this man burst in," he said, addressing his remarks to Quentin Harris. "I haven't yet been told why."

It was Tracy who answered. The dapper executive's handsome face was troubled. "I'm afraid you're in a pretty nasty mess this time, Ray," he said.

"What have I done?"

The partially bald man with the scrubby mustache came over and stood directly in front of Ray. His eyes, black and fathomless, were like drills. "Do you deny," he asked, "that you threatened Walter Keene yesterday? That you said you would break his head?" He hadn't been told yet, but Ray already knew the answer. The same hopeless trapped feeling he had experienced when the judge sentenced him to the penitentiary now numbed his muscles, took the starch from his spine.

"I had an argument with Keene yesterday," he said, trying to keep his voice firm. "Keene went out of his way to be insulting. I resented it, naturally. Is that a crime?"

"If it stopped at that, no," U. G. Flint said. His eyes pierced Ray steadily. "In this case, however…"

He turned abruptly to the tall, hatchet-faced plainclothes detective who seemed to be in charge of the police detail. "Lieutenant Lambert, I think you'd better show this man to the other end of the room."

Lambert took Ray by the arm. His fingers, twisted in the cloth of Rays work shirt, bit painfully into the flesh beneath. As they marched together around the row of laboratory benches, Ray heard Harris make some crack about confronting a criminal with the evidence of his crime.

Walter Keene was sitting at a small flat-topped desk halfway the length of the long laboratory. There was a thin pile of papers on the desk and one of Keene's hands lay across them. The other hung loosely by his side.

He was leaning back in the battered swivel chair, his wrinkled face unnaturally relaxed, his jaw dropped open. His beady eyes, too, were open wide, but their malicious glitter was gone. They were opaque now, glazed and dilated.

Ray had known even before he saw the man that Keene would be dead. What surprised him was the lack of any sign of violence about the body. There was no disfigurement, no wounds, not even any blood. If it were not for those dead eyes, and the sagging jaw, the laboratory assistant might simply be sitting back, resting from his work.

Ten feet from Keene's body, in an aisle between the laboratory benches, a police photographer was focusing his camera. Other men were busily engaged, dusting for fingerprints, making sketches, the whole varied routine of preliminary police investigation.

"What did you hit him with?" Lieutenant Lambert shot at Ray suddenly.

Ray said, "I didn't hit him with anything."

"How did you kill him, then?"

"Has he been killed?" Ray asked. "Maybe—"

"He looks dead, doesn't he?"

"Yes, but maybe he had a heart attack. Or…"

"Maybe he was figuring his income tax," Lambert said. "Perhaps when he saw the figures the shock was too great for him."

Tracy and Harris and LI. G. Flint had come down behind them. The laboratory people crowded silently in back.

"Do you deny having killed this man?" Flint asked.

"I didn't touch him. Last time I saw Walter Keene he was all right. It looks as if…couldn't he have died from natural causes?"

"He could have," Flint said, "but he didn't." He turned toward a small, white-haired man among the group near the body. "Dr. Roberts tells us this man's skull has been fractured."

Ray spoke hurriedly, without thinking. "Maybe he fell downstairs. He could have climbed back up here before…"

The Medical Examiner spoke decisively. "The head doesn't *look* injured but the skull has been smashed into several pieces, literally shattered to bits. It doesn't require an autopsy to know that this man couldn't have walked a step. Death must have been instantaneous."

"And that," Lieutenant Lambert of the Homicide Squad remarked with emphasis, "makes it *murder*." A feeling of utter despair swept over Ray. The mere fact of being involved in a murder investigation might be fatal so far as his future was concerned. A monthly report to the Parole Officer was a condition of his release from prison. It would take little to send him hack.

He pulled forward against Lambert's restraining hand, peering intently at the dead man's head and noting the bruises on Walter Keene's scalp, beneath the thin sandy hair. There were two small marks, one semicircular, a little smaller than a dime, the other a complete circle, twice as large as the first, red against the whiteness of the skin. Inside the circle was another mark shaped roughly like the letter T.

Lambert jerked back on Ray's arm. "What're you trying to do?"

"Nothing. Just looking."

"Take a *good* look at what you did, Locke! Maybe you'd like to confess now. It'll go easier with you."

"There's nothing to confess. Why do you want to make me the goat?"

Ashley spoke up from the rear. "You came barging into this laboratory yesterday, Locke. I should think you would have been ashamed even to show your face around here. You deliberately provoked an argument with Keene, made threats against his life. I heard it all myself."

"And you were hanging around last night," Quentin Harris added quickly. "I have my own secretary's statement to that effect."

Rays eyes searched the faces behind him for Jackie North. The pert little brunette was nowhere in sight.

"It would be interesting," he said, "to know what a girl from the general offices was doing inside the plant at two o'clock in the morning."

Tracy was looking hard at Harris. "Yes, Quentin. What *was* Miss North doing here?"

The bulky Assistant General Superintendent lowered his eyes. He seemed embarrassed. "I don't know."

Ray pressed his advantage. "And what was Glenn Cannon doing here with her?"

Tracy's gray-green eyes suddenly narrowed. "Cannon! *He* couldn't have been here." He turned to Bixler. "I gave explicit instructions that none of your men was to admit Cannon to the works without signed authorization from me!"

The company cop said, "I passed your order along, Mr. Tracy. I don't think none of my boys would have let him in. I'll check on it."

"Do that. And report to me."

"Cannon was here," Ray insisted. "At the lab. I saw him."

There was a flush of anger on Tracy's cheeks. "How about it, Harris? Did you allow that man—"

"I have never even seen Cannon, neither yesterday nor any other time." There was a ring of truth in Harris' statement. "Locke is lying."

"Cannon?" Flint said questioningly. "Is he the man..."

Harris said, "He's the man."

"We'll have to check on that girl of yours, too," Tracy said.

Ray fired another shot in his own defense. "When I left here last night, Walter Keene had gone up into the chemical lab. I was downstairs with Miss Dunne. She'll bear me out on that."

"I did see Locke go off past the machine shop," Clara Dunne's calm voice said. "I don't know where he went after that, of course."

"I went straight out Gate Number Six," Ray said. "You can check my card with the timekeeper."

"You can bet your neck we'll do that," Lambert promised. "You're still the guilty guy in my hook, pally—a convict on the loose with a grudge to settle."

Ray was regaining his confidence. "Ben Gaylord, you were around here, too, when I checked out last night. I saw you through a window of the machine shop."

Gaylord was standing near Christopher Ashley. "I worked until two-thirty," he said. "I went home from the machine shop without even coming back to the lab."

Ashley said, "You haven't yet told us what *you* were doing around here at two o'clock."

It shouldn't have caught Ray flat-footed, but it did. "I told Miss Dunne last night," he said. "I came to check on a melt at the Open Hearth."

He knew he had made a bad mistake when Harris said, "It'll be easy enough to verify that with Mr. Quirk."

The technical men from the homicide detail had finished their work and were packing up their paraphernalia.

"You can get on back to Headquarters," Lambert told them, "all except Jones and Reed. You fellows stick around with me until the meat-wagon gets here. Next thing I've got to get are statements from all these people."

Tracy glanced at U. G. Flint. "This is going to give us some more unfortunate publicity, General."

His attitude suggested that he, Ironton's top executive, was looking to the General for guidance.

The General was as tall as Lieutenant Lambert, but heavier. His heaviness was not that of fat, but rather the solidity of big bones and powerful muscles. His hair was jet black, without so much as a single gray or white hair. The shiny bald streak ran from his broad forehead to the back of his neck with the evenness of a swath cut through thick grass by a lawnmower.

"I'm going to ask that you fellows handle this case in a highly irregular manner," he said, addressing Lambert. "Don't bother to take the statements. I'll do it for you. In fact, I want to carry on the whole investigation myself."

Lambert demurred at once. "It's my job, Mr. Flint. The Commissioner—"

"The Commissioner will see things my way, I'm sure." The General's tone was smooth but positive. "I'll speak to him myself."

"But what will I..."

"You'll do nothing. Just stick around. Technically, of course, you're still handling everything, only I'll do the work for you. I'll ask your force to help with details. When the case is solved you'll get full credit. That's the way American-Consolidated Steel would like to handle it."

Lieutenant Lambert shrugged. "I guess that's that! What good would it do for eighty bucks a week to argue against two billion smackers?"

As the technical men trooped toward the stairs Lambert said, "Just one thing, Mr. Flint. Why don't you let me run in this bird Locke on suspicion? Chances are, he's guilty. If not,"—he hunched his thin shoulders expressively—"well, no harm's done."

The General's piercing eyes studied Ray coldly. The man was evidently a plenty tough cookie, Ray thought, but fortunately there seemed no particular prejudice either for or against him in the General's mind.

"Maybe he's guilty," the General said. "Maybe not. One thing's certain, however: at two o'clock this morning this laboratory must have been as crowded as Times Square on New Year's Eve." He frowned, then continued, "I'm going to have a little session with Locke first. Then I want to see some of these other people over at the office building. Suppose you come over to Mr. Tracy's office when you're ready, Lieutenant."

"Okay. I'll be there in about half an hour."

The General said something to Tracy in an undertone. Tracy nodded, then stepped out in front of the knot of Test Department employees, facing them.

"Everyone get back to work now," he said. "We've all got plenty to do and a lot of time's been lost already. The excitement's over."

"One thing more," he added as they began reluctantly to disperse. "Mr. U. G. Flint"—he nodded toward the General—"will want to talk privately with certain people among you about this unfortunate affair. I shall expect you all to cooperate with him to the utmost. Mr. Flint will have full and complete authority around this plant and nothing he desires to do is to be questioned by anyone."

Tracy, Harris and the General turned then to the stairs.

Over his shoulder the General said, "Bixler, you'd better bring Locke."

The huge company cop laid a heavy hand on Ray's shoulder. "You see what I mean, bud?" he suggested with an unpleasant grin. "Them boxcars meant just one wooden box!"

FOUR

Ashley's office, which the General had commandeered for his talk with Ray, was furnished only with a scarred, oak, flat-top desk, a single oak armchair, a steel filing cabinet, and an old black leather couch, vintage of the late nineteenth century. There was no carpet on the floor. The only wall decorations were a graph of steel production and the business cycle since 1850, a calendar with the picture of a pretty girl scantily clad, and a framed diploma showing that a Master of Science degree had been conferred on Christopher Ashley at Lehigh in 1913.

The General gestured to the chair at the side of the desk and Ray sat down. The General swung around and transfixed him with his shrewd, piercing eyes.

"Well, young man, you're in a very serious jam." The big man's tone was a simple statement of fact. It was not friendly, but neither was it hostile.

"I realize that, sir."

"For your own good," the General said, "it would be wise to tell me the exact truth."

"That's what I intend to do."

"You still deny you killed this man Keene?"

"I didn't know Keene was dead until I saw him upstairs just now."

"But you had good reason to kill him?"

Ray said, "No. Certainly not. You don't kill a man just for making a nasty crack."

"You threatened him."

"I threatened to beat him up. He did deserve a beating."

"You threatened his life. We have witnesses to that."

Ray's fingers picked at a roughness of the wood in the chair arm. "I was angry. I guess I did say something about breaking his head. I was just sounding off. I didn't mean it at all the way it sounds now."

The General placed the palm of his hand flat against the desk top, leaning his weight against it with the elbow bent. There were coarse black hairs on the man's wrist and on the back of his hand.

"When we sent for you," he went on, "you were up and dressed. Yet I understand you worked the night shift at the Open Hearth. It seems a bit peculiar that you weren't asleep, if your conscience was clear."

Ray shifted uncomfortably in his chair. "I have some rather peculiar habits about sleeping. I sleep only a couple of hours at night and make up for it by taking short naps during the day. It's a good routine to get into—gives you several extra hours a day. A man can do a lot in these additional hours…"

"Such as cracking the skull of someone you despise?" the General asked quietly.

The eagerness faded from Rays face. "You think I'm guilty, don't you?"

"I don't think anything—yet," the General said. "Snap judgments are dangerous. A man's judgment is only as good as his information."

"Well, that's what I was doing up and dressed when this plug-ugly Bixler barged in on me," Ray insisted. "I'd had my nap. I was reading, brushing up on the basic open hearth process."

The General began, "I understand—"

The ringing of the phone on the desk interrupted him. He reached out a big hand and took up the receiver. "Yes? Yes, Flint speaking. He did, eh? Well, that's something worth knowing! Keep it under your hat, please, until you hear from me."

He set the receiver back on its hook. When he turned again to Ray, there was a new sternness in his manner.

"That was Mr. Harris," he said. "He's checked with the people at the Open Hearth. They didn't send you over here last night."

Ray said nothing.

"You lied about that," the General accused. "What were you doing here then?"

Ray hesitated. "You know my background, sir?" he asked.

"To a limited extent. Mr. Harris informs me you're the man whose dishonesty was responsible for that railroad wreck."

Ray was thinking fast. If he told the truth it might cost him his chance to clear himself of the bribery charge. If he didn't, it might cost him his neck. He chose the lesser of the two evils and took the plunge.

"I was framed," he told the General. "I was absolutely innocent. I came to the lab last night because I wanted to look through the old Test Department records. I thought I might find something to help me prove what I've told everyone."

"What makes you think anything revealing—provided you're telling me the truth, of course—would still be around?" the General probed.

"It would have been risky destroying or altering the old test records," Ray replied. "Someone might have noticed and started asking questions.

Anyway, why bother? Cannon and I were the only ones who would have been interested, and we were safely tucked away, God knows!"

The General's face was as expressionless as granite. His eyes burned steadily into Ray's with an intensity which made the younger man flinch.

"You asked for the truth and I've given it to you," Ray cried out. "I was accused of accepting a bribe from the Chief Inspector of this plant. But I was as innocent of that charge as you are."

"You were convicted," the General said finally. "There was *documentary proof!*"

"Why would I do a petty thing like that?" Ray argued desperately. "My father was a highly successful research engineer. He'd trained me from childhood for a career in research metallurgy, particularly the metallurgy of iron and steel. I worked in the mills on summer vacations. I had training in metallurgical engineering at the very finest technical university. I was simply rounding out my training with a year as Material Inspector for the railroad. Then I was going in with my father. Would I throw away all my future prospects for a few lousy dollars in graft?"

"There was once a man named Judas who sold out for a handful of silver," the General said quietly.

"I'm no Judas," Ray said, "and I'm not an utter and complete fool!"

The General leaned back in the swivel chair and regarded Ray unwinkingly. Ray could feel his pulse throbbing in his throat with suffocating intensity. Not until the silence had begun to grow intolerable did the General speak.

"I had an idea," he said, "that your visit here last night might be for exactly the reason you've outlined. That's why I wanted to talk with you alone. And it's one of the principal reasons I asked the police to keep hands off until I had time to do a little investigation of my own. I don't care to have the company's dirty linen washed in public."

U. G. Flint took a cigar from his pocket, trimmed the end with deliberation. Not until he had it alight, did he continue. "This matter of dishonesty in tests of steel at the Ironton Works is of the most vital importance to my people," he went on. His manner had changed, becoming surprisingly confidential. "The reputation of American-Consolidated Steel is a matter of considerable more importance than the death of an obscure chemist or even a hundred chemists for that matter."

Ray let out his breath in a sigh of relief. "Then you do believe me?"

"Say, rather, that I haven't yet found reason to disbelieve you," the General amended. "What I'm trying to do is get all the facts. I want you to tell me, now, exactly what happened when you came here last night. Don't omit a single detail, no matter how unimportant it may seem to you."

Ray followed instructions to the letter, even to relating the injury he had unwittingly inflicted upon the unoffending laboratory cat. When he had finished, the General sat a while in silence, meditatively watching the smoke circling upward from his cigar.

"Entirely too many people were milling around this place at two o'clock this morning," he remarked finally. "Maybe an excessive amount of overtime is required from Test Department personnel. That would indicate faulty organization: a management problem. Or else"—his piercing eyes hooded suddenly—"or else we have a bunch of scurvy scoundrels and sanctimonious sons-of-sea-cooks on the payroll."

Abruptly he stabbed a blunt forefinger at Ray. "One thing I want to impress upon you strongly: *Say nothing to anyone about your reason for being at the laboratory last night.* Not to the police, not to your department heads, not even to Mr. Tracy if he should ask you. Is that quite clear?"

A crushing weight seemed to be removed from Ray's chest. "I understand," he said quietly. "It's the last thing I want to talk about."

The General said, "Good. You may just happen to be useful to me, Locke. For your own good it's very important that you follow my instructions. Just remember what Eve said and…"

His manner indicated he was about to terminate the interview. Ray spoke quickly. "I've been doing a lot of thinking about the manner in which Walter Keene was killed and the fact that his skull was smashed into several pieces. Did you notice the marks on his scalp?"

The General's bushy black eyebrows lifted. "I did indeed. What about them?"

"It looked to me," Ray said, "like either the mark of an inspector's hammer stamp or a swage."

"I don't quite follow you," Flint said. "I'm not a steel man, you see."

"Oh, I thought you were." Ray was amazed. "Well, it's like this. A hammer stamp is used for marking test pieces and accepted orders. When an inspector from some large buyer of steel like a railroad is notified that a shipment is ready, he comes to the plant and looks over the material for surface defects. He also picks specimens at random for laboratory tests.

"These specimens are turned in the machine shop to the standard size and shape for breaking in a machine for determining tensile strength. So he can be sure the test piece actually came from the material he looked at, the inspector marks his specimen with a small hammer he carries with him."

"The hammer has a distinctive mark?"

"Yes, sir. The head of the hammer is made of tool steel with a die that cuts into softer steel. Each company has its own identifying mark. In the case of the New York, St. Louis and Pacific, the mark consists of a capital T in a circle, standing for the road's trademark, Transcontinental Line."

"Go ahead," Flint said. "I'm listening."

"However, a blow with a hand hammer hard enough to cause death would probably have smashed a hole in the man's skull," Ray pointed out, "not cracked the bones in several places, as the doctor said was the case. Moreover the mark on Keene's scalp was much larger, maybe twice as large as the hammer stamp. It could have been done by a swage. That would have caused the mark and crushed his head without any external evidence."

"What's a swage?" the General cut in.

"A swage," Ray explained, "is a tool used in metal working operations, particularly forging. It's held on top of the work and struck a heavy blow. The work is therefore forced into the shape of the swage. That's the way the work is given its finished form."

"Hmmm."

"I happen to know," Ray finished, "that driving axles, truck axles, main and side rods and other miscellaneous forgings made to the specifications of the Transcontinental are always marked with the road's emblem. The swages used for that road's work all have its identifying symbol."

The General slapped his hand against the desk top. "Locke, maybe you've got something!"

"Could be nothing but imagination," Ray admitted. "In order to kill Walter Keene by covering his head with a swage and pounding it under a steam hammer, the operator would have had to be very skillful or he'd have beaten the man's head to a pulp."

"It could have been done, however?"

"A really expert hammer man can break a watch crystal under his hammer without hurting the watch itself."

U. G. Flint raised his powerful hulk from Ashley's swivel chair. "I respect ideas, Locke," he said. "Even a wild idea is better than none. Most people have no ideas; they never use their brains. You're going to take me right now to the place where they use these swages. We'll soon see whether your idea is a good one or not."

But in the short hallway outside the office, the General turned back. "You wait here," he ordered. "I've got a phone call to make first."

Ashley's door shut behind Flint. Ray was wet with clammy perspiration.

In about three minutes the General was hack. "Let's go," he said briskly.

The forge, or hammer shop, was a long building with a dirt floor. Like Vulcan's workshop it was cavern-like, gloomy, peopled with grimy, sweating gnomes. And like the workshop of the mythical Roman god, it was a place of flame and smoke, of blinding brilliance and deep contrasting black shadows.

Along the walls near the shop entrance, sinewy men worked small glowing bits of iron by hand, as in an ordinary blacksmith shop. In the center space, and running the length of the long building, were the steam hammers. They were of all sizes, ranging from little two-hundred-pounders to the sixteen-thousand-pound monsters used to reduce alloy steel ingots to billets for drop forging.

Ray Locke stopped near a big hammer about a hundred and fifty feet in from the entrance nearest the testing laboratory. On the earth at one side of the hammer, a pile of black, rectangular-shaped billets, was stacked like cordwood. On the hammer's other side were billets which had been beaten under the hammer to a circular shape. Ray stooped and examined one of the round shapes.

He pointed. "Look."

Stamped into the black metal about five inches from the end, were a series of numbers ending with the circled T Ray had mentioned.

"Normalized carbon-vanadium for engine axles," Ray said. "These will be rough turned before they are delivered to the railroad's own shops for finishing. Specifications require each forging to be marked with heat number, part number, test number, and the like. They also require that a black collar of metal be left on the forging, with these numbers and the inspector's personal identifying stamp. You can see that these numbers have been put on by hand with dies, but the road's emblem is cut into the billet by the swage. There is no inspector's mark, so evidently these forgings have not yet been submitted for inspection."

The General was bending over the steel, following Ray's index finger along the marks. "So far, so good," be murmured. "Now let's see if we can find the swage that might have been used on Keene."

Ray picked over the tools beside the hammer frame. He selected a piece of metal, rounded at one end to form a handle, flaring into a heavy curved section at the other.

"We want one like this," he said. "See, this is the way it works." He reached for a lever like a locomotive's throttle bar at the side of the towering hammer frame. A five-ton block of steel swung downward, then up again, pulsating restlessly, poised over the massive hundred-ton anvil beneath.

"You hold the swage like this," he said, demonstrating. The tool was thrust between the hammer and anvil, curved portion downward. "A few ten-thousand-pound blows and the hot metal shapes up quickly enough." Ray grimaced. "You can imagine what would happen to a man's head!"

A burly giant in soiled work clothes approached them from the rear of the shop. "Leave that hammer be," he ordered gruffly. "What d'ya think y're doin'?" Ray recognized the same big man he had seen with Gaylord in the machine shop early that morning. He released the throttle. The hammer swung back to the top of the guide frame and stayed there.

The giant's eyes were noting U. G. Flint's expensively tailored, dark gray business suit. "If you're the railroad inspector," he said, "we ain't ready for you yet. Had to pull my men off on a rush job."

"I'm not the railroad inspector," Flint said.

"Then get away from this stuff," the big man ordered. "You ain't got no business messin' around."

"Who are you?" the General inquired.

"I'm Al Sisco, the foreman of this here hammer shop, that's who! Now you guys scram outta here!"

Very quietly the General said, "I'm here by authority of Mr. Leonard Tracy and the management of the company in New York. I intend to stay here until I get good and ready to leave. If you care to start something…"

Sisco didn't. The General's positive manner overawed the man. But he didn't like it. All the time Ray and the General remained in the forge shop, the big man lingered near the next hammer in the row, watching them with a sullen, scowling stare.

Ray was now eyeing the swage closely. "This can't be the one!" he said. "This is a roughing tool. There's no circle T mark on this one."

The General fingered the other tools beside the hammer frame. In a moment he gave an exclamation of satisfaction and straightened with another swage in his hand.

"Looks as if you were absolutely right, Locke. This is where Keene got it, all right."

On the inner curve of the tool, the circle with its T was plain. A slight brownish discoloration stained the edges of the circular die, about as much as two drops of drying blood would leave. And caught on the crossbar of the T was a single, short, sandy hair. Unless one looked carefully, neither the stain nor the hair would have been visible.

"Lucky for me," Ray observed, "they weren't working this hammer today." To himself he was thinking exultantly, "Bixler was wrong."

Flint said, "This will interest Lieutenant Lambert. We'll take it along with us to the laboratory and lock it up somewhere for safe keeping."

Ray turned to follow the General and as he did so, a glint of gold from the dirt floor caught his eyes. He stooped.

It wasn't gold; just brass. A fragment about an inch long, like a hollow truncated pyramid, with sharp ragged edges, it looked as if it were a corner broken from a brass box.

Delicate lines, made by some kind of hand tool, were etched on the yellow metal in an indistinguishable design which twisted from one straight segment around the box corner to the other. Ray could not determine what the design was supposed to represent, since the piece was so small.

What, he wondered briefly, was a thing like this doing on the floor of the hammer shop? Heavy steel forgings, such as locomotive axles, were the only materials usually shaped under the hammers. Brass was distinctly out of place.

He thrust the bit of metal into his pocket, forgot it as he hurried to catch up with U. G. Flint already a dozen paces ahead of him.

There was a new note in the Generals deep voice, a note of distinct friendliness. "You know, Locke, you've really been very helpful. I think you're being wasted on the Open Hearth. I should like to have you on the Test Department payroll."

Ray said, "I'd like it, too, sir. But Mr. Tracy didn't feel it wise to put me there."

"Tracy will," U. G. Flint said decisively, "I feel sure, change his mind about that."

FIVE

Leonard Tracy was not in his luxurious private office when Ray and the General reached the Administration Building. He had gone, Tracy's secretary informed them, to supervise the blowing in of a new blast furnace.

Almost as soon as the General had seated himself in Tracy's blue leather swivel chair, Lieutenant Lambert walked in. He gave Ray a quick, unfriendly glance.

"We've checked Locke's statement," he told the General, "that he went to the laboratory last night on an errand for the Open Hearth foreman."

"Here it comes!" Ray thought, and braced himself mentally. Lambert had discovered his lie, thereby putting him squarely on the spot he had dreaded.

U. G. Flint's insistence that Ray say nothing, even to the police, of his real motive for visiting the laboratory was going to put him in an even worse jam.

"I felt sure Locke was lying," the homicide detective went on. "The boys at the Open Hearth could have checked a carbon analysis by phone." His hard eyes studied Ray intently. "And it was a good hour after you were supposed to go off shift."

Ray decided to stick to his guns. Whatever happened, he would follow U. G. Flint's instructions. He had a hunch the General was his best—maybe his *only*—hope of clearing himself from suspicion.

"I'm not a clock watcher," he told Lambert quietly. "When my boss asks me to do something extra, I do it."

"That's what the head guy told me," Lambert admitted surprisingly. "Said they'd taken an extra sample and sent you over to the lab with it."

Ray hoped his astonishment did not show in his face. The General's features were devoid of expression and the big man did not meet Ray's eyes. "Then he had a perfectly legitimate reason for being there," he said to Lambert. "Locke's story strikes me as being straightforward. For the time being, at least, I think we'd better give him the benefit of the doubt."

"I guess you're right," Lambert admitted reluctantly. "But don't think you're not still under suspicion," he added to Ray. "Your record and your threat against Keene still carry a lot of weight with me."

The General said, "I've asked the various Test Department supervisors to come over. They're waiting outside now."

"Let's have them in," Lambert agreed, "but one at a time. Locke, you can go now. Stick around, though, where I can get you when I want you."

"I think," the General said as Ray got to his feet, "it might be advisable for Locke to remain here while we talk to these people."

Lambert shrugged. "If you wish, Mr. Flint." He did not question the General's purpose.

"I do." The General flipped a switch on Tracy's inter-office communication system. "Will you ask Mr. Ashley to come in, please?"

The secretary's voice replied promptly. "Yes, sir."

"We'll take the department head, first," the General said. "Better for organization morale than to keep him cooling his heels."

Ashley came through the door from the anteroom. The Engineer of Tests seemed definitely ill at ease. He stroked his small, pointed beard nervously, standing awkwardly in front of the big, circular desk like a schoolboy about to receive a reprimand from the principal.

The General waved the man to one of the deep blue leather chairs. Ashley perched gingerly on its edge, waiting in silence for Flint to speak.

"Unfortunate affair," the General said conversationally. "Too bad we have to take your time and the time of your supervisors. I guess you're all pretty rushed these days?"

"Dreadfully so," Ashley agreed. "Like everyone else we're short-handed. Now that Keene is gone…"

"Keene was a valuable man?"

"He'd been with us a long time," Ashley said. "Shouldered a lot of Clara Dunne's detail work. I don't know what she'll do now."

The General trimmed the end from a cigar. "Your people put in a lot of overtime?"

"They've had to lately, since we run one shift instead of three."

"What time do you start in the mornings?"

"We have someone on duty all the time," Ashley explained, "in the chemical lab, that is. We cut two shifts on the physical lab, however. We simply didn't have the manpower. Of course we have our inspectors in the various mills all night, but the physical lab itself opens now at eight A.M."

"And runs until when?"

"Five, theoretically." Ashley was growing more at ease. He leaned back in the armchair, stopped plucking at his wispy beard. "Actual hours don't mean much to us. We're all salaried employees, you know, white-collar workers. We have no union to look after us."

"Even so," the General suggested, "sticking around until two or three in the morning seems rather drastic. Is that sort of thing customary?"

"I wouldn't say so. Occasionally—"

Lieutenant Lambert cut him short. "Your laboratory last night was lousy with people."

Ashley didn't reply. His eyes were roaming Tracy's big, elaborate office, with avid curiosity. This was the first time, evidently, that he had been inside the Ironton czar's private sanctum.

Flint said, "I understand you were not here yourself last night."

"No. I wasn't."

"What time did you check out?" Lambert asked. "Shortly after five."

"Then you didn't know about Keene until…"

"One of the girls upstairs, a chemist, found him this morning," Ashley explained. "She was the first one in. She came running down and informed Gaylord. I didn't get in until half an hour later."

"Is there anything you can tell us at first hand? Think carefully."

Ashley stroked his heard a moment in silence, then he shook his head. "Nothing you don't already know."

"Can you think of any enemies Keene might have had? Anyone with a motive which might have led to murder?"

"This man right here!" Ashley nodded toward Ray. "Every time Locke comes around the Ironton Works we seem to have trouble."

Lambert bobbed his head in agreement. The General, however, brushed the remark aside.

"That's rather indefinite," he said. "Why should Locke have it in for Keene? Was there any past feeling between the two men, to your knowledge?"

Ashley said, "No," reluctantly. "But they had a serious argument yesterday. I told you that."

"I know. It appears that Keene took it upon himself to make certain gratuitous, insulting remarks, remarks any man would have resented."

"Locke threatened to break Keene's head," Ashley insisted stubbornly. "And this morning Keene's head was broken."

Lambert murmured, "Quite true!"

The General looked at Ashley searchingly. "Then, you can't add anything that might help us." He summed it up, "You weren't anywhere around the plant last night yourself. You—"

"Where were you last night?" Lambert cut in. "Just for the record."

Ashley answered very quickly, almost as if he had anticipated the question. "I went into the city to the public library. Spent the whole evening there with Stanton Masey's book *Micrographic Analysis of Austenitic Steels.*"

Lambert grunted. "Nice entertaining reading!"

"One of the librarians down there, a Miss Jackson, will probably remember seeing me last evening," Ashley added. "I go there fairly often."

"You weren't at the library at two in the morning, were you?" Flint demanded suddenly.

"Of course not, sir. I left the library when it closed at nine-thirty, and went home to bed."

"Did anyone see you there? Are you married?"

"No, sir." Ashley's absent-minded brown eyes held a startled look. "I have a bachelor apartment in town." He mentioned a city address. "I hope you don't..."

"I don't think anything," the General said brusquely. "I'm just trying to get the facts—*all* the facts."

"I've told you everything I can." Ashley shifted uncomfortably in the deep soft chair. "I wasn't anywhere near the plant last night. My card at Gate Six will show the time I checked in and out."

"Just one more thing," Flint said. "What do you suppose your former Chief Inspector, Glenn Cannon, was doing around the lab last night? He might have had good reason for wanting to knock off this man Keene."

Ashley sniffed. "I don't think Cannon was in the plant."

"Locke says he saw him."

"Locke says a lot of things," Ashley retorted curtly. "The word of a convicted felon means nothing."

"I'm sorry you feel that way because you may have to work with Locke."

"What do you mean!"

"I have reason to believe that Locke may be transferred to work in your testing laboratory."

"I don't want him in my department," Ashley said.

"Nevertheless," the General insisted, "he is quite likely to he placed there. And if he does come under your supervision, you're to give him a fair break. Do I make myself clear on that point?"

Ashley gulped. "Yes, sir."

"That's all for now, then."

As Ashley walked toward the door, the General flipped the switch on the desk box. "Send in Mr. Gaylord next, please."

"Didn't get much to help us from that bearded old goat," Lambert remarked.

"You can't kill a pig every day in the week," the General observed serenely, "and cast the bollix to feed the poor."

Benjamin Gaylord was wearing the faded, clay-brown suit which Ray had seen the day before. It was evidently his customary work costume. He looked like a neat but threadbare cadaver.

The man's diffidence, as he came into the big paneled office, was evident. His eyes, deep sunk into his skull-like head, darted around in a quick look before he took the chair to which the General waved him.

"I understand," the General said, "that you rank next to Mr. Ashley in the Test Department."

"Yes, sir."

"Just what is the nature of your work, Gaylord?"

"As Chief Inspector," Gaylord said, "I am responsible for the condition of all steel that leaves this plant."

"Just what does that mean?"

"We have inspectors constantly checking each step of manufacture," Gaylord explained, "from furnaces to finished product. For instance, we have men in the plate mill who measure and gauge each plate to see that it has been rolled and cut to the proper size. And the products of all the various other rolling mills are similarly examined to make sure they are free from surface defects and imperfections. All such inspectors report to me.

Flint's black, bushy brows drew together slightly. "I thought you told me," he remarked to Ray Locke, "that this sort of work was done by inspectors employed by big buyers of steel products?"

Gaylord gave a death's head smile. "Oh, we have outside inspectors around the mills every day," he explained. "Part of our job is to help these fellows to make their own tests and to keep them happy. But the biggest part of our work, naturally, is keeping tabs on our own steel. It doesn't help the sales department if we ship inferior goods to our customers. If something's wrong with our product, we want to catch it first."

"You don't always, do you?"

"With the tonnage Ironton turns out, I think we have a fairly small percentage of rejected material."

Lieutenant Lambert said, "Let's see now if I get this Test Department set-up straight. If I were in charge of your open hearth furnaces, say, and I wanted to check the amount of carbon in a certain batch of steel, I'd come to you. Is that right?"

"Not exactly. Chemical analysis would be Miss Dunne's province. She has charge of the chemists. I handle everything except the chemical end. My man would take the test specimen, or would help an outside inspector take it. But the chemist who made the actual analysis would be Miss Dunne's helper."

Lambert said, "I get it now."

"Keeps you right busy these days, I guess," the General suggested casually.

"You can say that again. This place is a madhouse lately."

"Put in a lot of overtime? I mean yourself, personally."

"Almost every day," Gaylord admitted. "Couldn't keep up with the work if I didn't."

"You were here pretty late last night, weren't you?"

For the first time Gaylord seemed to sense the direction the questioning was taking. "Last night was unusual," he said hurriedly. "I had some special tests to arrange for today. I stayed very late on that account."

"What kind of tests?"

"Axles for one of the railroads." Gaylord gave Ray a sidelong glance. His almost colorless wisp of brown mustache twitched slightly.

"What do you know about this business of Walter Keene?" Lambert demanded suddenly.

"Nothing at all," Gaylord said promptly. "I was nowhere near the laboratory."

"Locke says he saw you in the machine shop talking with a couple of men. That's not far from the Test Department building."

"Right next door," Gaylord admitted. He had lost his air of confidence, spoke more slowly and cautiously. "But I didn't come back into the laboratory after I'd finished arranging the tests."

"What time was it when you left the machine shop?"

"Two-thirty. I remember looking at my watch and thinking I was going to get a very short night's rest."

"Where did you go from the machine shop?"

"Home. Directly home."

"Who were these two men Locke saw you with?"

"Just a couple of men around the plant."

"Give us a more direct answer, please," the General said sharply. "We will want to talk with those men. This, you know, is a murder investigation."

Gaylord's eyes behind his rimless glasses were apprehensive. "Certainly you don't think *I* had anything to do with Keene's death?"

"You might have," Lambert said bluntly. "That's what we're trying to find out."

"I hardly knew the man," Gaylord protested. "He was a chemist. I didn't come in contact with his work."

"No one's accused you," Lambert said. "We were just asking."

"Who were the two men?" the General asked again.

Gaylord hesitated. For some reason he seemed reluctant to mention names. "One of them, a big fellow named Sisco, is the hammer shop foreman," he said finally. "His men are working on the axle order."

"And the other one?"

"Pete Kosleck, a machinist. He was turning up test pieces for the railroad inspector to pull at the lab this morning."

The General tried a new tack. "What do you know about Glenn Cannon?"

Gaylord looked bewildered. "Cannon used to be Chief Inspector." Again he darted a sidelong glance at Ray.

"You formerly worked for him?"

"Yes, sir."

"And after he...after he left, you got his job?"

"Yes, sir."

"What do you suppose he could have been doing around the laboratory at two o'clock this morning?"

Gaylord was visibly shaken. "It's impossible that Cannon could have been at the lab."

"Why impossible?"

"Because Glenn's...he's a long way off," Gaylord finished lamely.

"You heard Locke say he saw Cannon at the laboratory last night."

Gaylord faced Ray directly then. "You must have been mistaken, Ray. You must have seen someone who looked like Cannon."

"It was Glenn," Ray said positively. "I ought to know what Glenn Cannon looks like."

The General switched the subject. "Do you know of anyone who might have wanted to kill Keene?"

Very promptly Gaylord said, "Yes, sir."

"Who?"

"'Windpipe' Bixler for one. He had a kid brother working in the chemical lab a short time back. Bixler got him the job, of course. Through Clara—Miss Dunne. But the kid was worthless, and Walter Keene was responsible for having Clara fire him. Bixler made quite a bit of talk about it and threatened to 'get' Walter."

"I see."

"Mr. Quentin Harris made some queer remarks about Keene quite recently, too," Gaylord volunteered. "I got it from one of the girls at the Exec offices."

"Sounds interesting. Tell me about it."

"It's hearsay," Gaylord admitted, "but I understand Harris was here in Mr. Tracy's office with someone, I don't know who. It wasn't Tracy, though. Anyhow, Harris raised his voice suddenly and said, 'Someone ought to take a little stick and kill Walter Keene.'"

"What else?"

"That's all I know about it."

The General said, "Well, that's informative. What else can you tell us?"

"I can't think of anything else, sir."

There was a little more conversation. Unlike Ashley, Gaylord made no reference to the argument between Ray Locke and the former laboratory assistant.

When the General finally told Gaylord he might go, the tightly stretched skin of the man's bony face seemed visibly to loosen. He hurried from the office with evident relief.

After the Chief Inspector had left the room, the General spoke to Lambert. "With your permission, Lieutenant, I'd like to give a few instructions to those men you left at the laboratory."

Lambert said, "Certainly, Mr. Flint. Give them whatever orders you wish."

The General spoke into the intercommunication system. "Please get me the laboratory on the telephone."

A moment later the phone jingled and he lifted the receiver. "Are the two men from the city police department still there? I'd like to speak to one of them."

A moment later he said, "Who is this? Jones? This is Mr. Flint. The Lieutenant wants you to do a little job for him. Yes. Is Reed there, too? Good. Here's what he wants you to do. One of you go over to the forge shop and get hold of the foreman, Al Sisco. The other go to the machine shop and locate a man by the name of Kosleck, a lathe operator. He wants you to check with each of these men about what they were doing with the steel company Chief Inspector at about two o'clock this morning. And do it before Gaylord has a chance to talk with them. Right? Yes. That's all."

He put back the receiver on its cradle and swung back to Lambert. "Maybe there's something there and maybe not. But Gaylord was around the laboratory at about the same time Keene was killed, if the Medical Examiner's timing means anything."

SIX

The General cast his half-smoked cigar into Tracy's fireplace and rose to his feet with punctilious politeness as Clara Dunne came into the room. He bent slightly at the hips, a courtly gesture reminiscent of the Old South.

The attractive, powerfully built Chief Chemist did not show the same awe of Tracy's rich surroundings as Ashley and Gaylord had exhibited. She seemed, in fact, as completely at ease as if the big office were her own little two-by-four cubbyhole on the second floor of the Test Department building.

The General waited until she had seated herself before dropping his weight into the desk chair again. He leaned forward then, eyeing Clara Dunne appraisingly.

"The death of your assistant must be a considerable shock to you, Miss Dunne," he began.

"I don't know that I'm exactly shocked," Clara said, "but I'll certainly be frightfully handicapped. It's like losing my right arm."

"Keene was a valuable assistant?"

"He took a tremendous amount of detail from my shoulders. He'd been around the laboratory even longer than I. By handling routine matters he enabled me to devote a considerable amount of my time to training green help. We have a great many inexperienced girls at the laboratory these days."

"You have a very important position for a woman," the General remarked.

"Fair." There was a note of dissatisfaction in her voice.

"You're extremely modest," the General said. "I should think it would take unusual competence to assume responsibility for the entire chemical division of a plant this size."

"I have a Master's degree from M.I.T.," Clara told him. She did not say it in a boastful way. "The work in our laboratory is fairly cut-and-dried. Most of it could be handled by anyone with a couple of years college chemistry. It's primarily simple quantitative and qualitative analysis."

"But it requires executive ability."

"I suppose so," she said disinterestedly.

The General glanced at Lambert and then at Ray Locke. "I suppose I'm getting to be an old fogey," he said, "but somehow I can never quite get used to the idea of women around steel mills. Such heavy industry seems essentially a man's job."

Ray was wondering about the General's age. Not more than early forties, he judged, in spite of the man's partial baldness.

Clara Dunne said, "I was brought up in the steel business. It has no terrors for me."

"Indeed?" The General's tone was politely inquiring.

She said, "My father started as a blacksmith. He worked up to superintendent of a small metal-working establishment. When the first World War broke, he bought out the business. I used to play around his shop when I was a kid."

Her face clouded. "I thought then that I'd manage the plant for him some day, build it up and up…" Her voice trailed off, then stopped.

"But you changed your mind," the General suggested. "You decided to be a chemist instead."

"My father lost his business in the big wind, the 1932 depression. He didn't live long after that. I had tough sledding even to put myself through school."

"1932, lots of people remember *that* year!" The General cleared his throat. "Well, to get back to Walter Keene. You were present, I understand, during the argument between him and Locke."

"That's right." Clara Dunne turned her eyes to Ray. There was no warmth in her look and no coldness. Her gaze was entirely impersonal. 'Walter Keene went out of his way to insult Mr. Locke. Mr. Locke tried to avoid a scene, but Walter wouldn't drop it. Finally Mr. Locke threatened to hit him. I stopped the quarrel."

"What was the argument about?" Lambert cut in.

"Why, Walter was making nasty cracks about—"

The General interrupted hastily. "Never mind. I don't think that's pertinent to the matter at hand."

A red flush crept into Lieutenant Lambert's lean cheeks. The police officer half opened his mouth, then thought better of it. He subsided sulkily against the cushions of his chair.

"I don't blame Mr. Locke," Clara Dunne said. "If I were a man and someone talked to me that way I'd knock his front teeth loose."

Ray said, "Thanks, Clara!"

The General took no notice of either Ray or the sullen Lambert.

"You told us over at the laboratory that you saw Locke go away from the test building while Keene was still around the laboratory?"

"He went off around the corner of the machine shop," Clara repeated.

"What happened after that?"

"I didn't stay around much longer myself," Clara said. "It was very late."

"Is it customary for you to work so late?"

"Not *that* late, but we've been awfully rushed the last few weeks. I've been getting steadily behind in my paper work. I thought last night would be a good time to catch up." She gave a disgusted little laugh. "I picked a good night, all right!"

"So you cleaned up your paper work and then went home?"

"I did *not* get caught up," she corrected. "There was more work than I thought. After the interruption, I realized I couldn't finish even if I worked all night, so I stopped."

"What time was it when you left the laboratory?"

"I didn't notice particularly. Around two, I think."

"That's just about the time the Medical Examiner fixes Keene's death."

She shrugged her chunky shoulders expressively. "What was Keene doing when you left?" the General asked.

"Something in the back part of the lab, I don't know exactly what. He was on night duty, you see. Supposed to be there until eight this morning and then off for twenty-four hours."

The General said, "Whom else did you see around the building before you left?"

"No one. That is, not just when I left."

"How about Gaylord?"

"He was in about eleven," Clara said. "He went out then and I didn't see him again the rest of the evening."

"Mr. Locke insists he saw the former Chief Inspector, Cannon, downstairs near Ashley's office. You knew Cannon, I presume?"

"I knew him, of course. But if he was around the plant last night it's news to me."

"What about Mr. Tracy's secretary, Miss Jacqueline North? She was there when you and Keene came down."

Clara said, "Yes. She and Mr. Locke were together."

"And Locke left before she did?"

"Miss North, if that's her name, went off right after Mr. Locke had gone."

"You don't know Miss North?"

"Never saw her before."

"Peculiar you wouldn't know the big boss' secretary," Flint observed.

"Why?" Clara Dunne asked calmly. "An office girl practically never comes inside the plant. We have no contact with any of the office employees—except, of course, the big shots, the superintendents."

"Then what was Miss North doing here last night, particularly at such a late hour?"

"You'd better ask her," Clara said. "She made no explanations to me last night."

"Didn't you ask?"

"I rather thought she came with Mr. Locke," Clara said. "As a matter of fact, she left right after he did. To tell the truth, I wasn't particularly interested. We have so many people around the lab all the time. And I don't mind saying I was upset last night. It bothers me to get so much behind in my work."

U. G. Flint sat for a moment without speaking. His big, blunt fingers drummed restlessly on Tracy's desk pad.

Then he said, "Miss Dunne, you strike me as being a young woman of considerable ability. I think you have a mind and know how to use it. Suppose you were sitting on my side of this desk. Where would you look for the murderer of Walter Keene?"

Very coolly, Clara Dunne said, "Thank you for the compliment, Mr. Flint, but I'm afraid I wouldn't be able to do much on this case. There are too many people who might have killed Walter!"

"Too many?" The General's eyes lighted up with sudden interest. "You mean Keene had a great many enemies?"

"No," she said. "I don't know if Walter had any enemies at all. But this is a very large plant. More than twenty thousand people are employed at Ironton. Any one of them could have killed Walter."

"Don't you think it likely that Keene's murderer was someone who knew him rather well? Someone, probably, closely associated with him at the Test Department in the course of his daily work?"

She considered a moment before replying. "In other words, you think the murderer is another employee of the Test Department? That *could* be true, naturally. But, then again, some hunkie from a loading gang might have come in and hit Walter over tire head."

"Considering the fact that there are three shifts during the twenty-four hours," the General pointed out, "only about a third of the twenty thousand would have been in the works at the time of Keene's murder. That cuts your number of suspects by roughly twelve thousand, right away."

"Any of the others could have come back into the plant on their own time if they'd wanted to," Clara pointed out. "I still think you've got one chance in twenty thousand of finding the person who killed Walter."

The General slapped his hand smartly against the desk top. "I can't agree with you, Miss Dunne!"

Clara Dunne's plump, pretty face crinkled in a smile. "I don't care whether you agree or not. It's still my opinion. You asked me and I've told you."

Ray Locke drew in his breath sharply. The pert comeback of the stocky Chief Chemist had bordered closely upon impudence.

U. G. Flint, however, did not take offense. "You don't realize it, Miss Dunne," he boomed, "but you've made this rather sordid affair vastly more interesting to me. I cannot fail now to find the murderer. Odds of twenty thousand-to-one against my success are a challenge I could never overlook. I thank you sincerely."

He got to his feet and bent again slightly at the hips, a signal that the interview was terminated.

Ray's fingers closed upon the dice in his vest pocket. When he glanced at them they showed a five and a two. "A natural!" he said aloud and snapped his fingers.

* * * *

The General spoke again briefly into the intercommunication box.

"I'm sorry," Jackie North's voice floated back. "Mr. Harris is out in the plant just now with Mr. Tracy."

"All right," said the General. "Suppose you step in yourself for a few moments."

He flipped the switch and tilted back in the desk chair.

"I'm quite surprised at Miss Dunne's attitude," he said speculatively. "It was distinctly on the defeatist side, and Ed have sworn she was anything but the frustrated type."

Lieutenant Lambert grinned sardonically. "Maybe she's been disappointed in love."

Somehow the idea of Clara Dunne eating her heart out with unrequited love struck Ray as ludicrous. The muscular little Chief Chemist was always so self-contained and efficient he simply couldn't picture her in a setting of moonlight and kisses.

Not that she was unattractive. But Ray had a swift mental picture of Clara Dunne cooking breakfast eggs as she would heat a beaker of hydrochloric acid in an analysis of carbon-vanadium drillings. The idea of Clara Dunne, complete with laboratory coat, in the kitchenette of a three-room apartment seemed incongruous.

The General spoke into the desk box again. "Miss North! We're waiting for you."

There was no answer.

"Go and see what's keeping her," he said to Ray with swift impatience. "We want to finish this questioning today, not next month."

Ray opened the connecting door to Harris' office. He gave a startled exclamation.

"Something's happened to Miss North!"

The girl lay on the floor halfway between her desk and the door. Her dark hair was a glossy fan against the green of the office rug. The red-framed glasses, fallen from her nose, lay on the floor just beyond her outflung hand.

The General and Lambert came through the door as Ray went down on one knee beside the prostrate girl. He slipped his arm around her slim shoulders, and carried her over to the leather couch near Harris' desk. She was limp and surprisingly inert.

U. G. Flint was peering over Rays back at Jackie. She was breathing rapidly, but her eyes were tightly closed.

"Not hurt!" Lambert diagnosed. "Fainted."

"Watch out!" the General warned suddenly. "Her glasses."

The big man retrieved the red rims almost from under Lambert's feet.

"We'll put these away fc [...] Vhere's the case?"

He stepped to Jacki [...] r, then another. The General picked up the g [...] d open the snap.

In another moment [...] de Lambert. "Look here!" he said. In his har [...] c of the cheap nickel variety sold at any five-: [...] blue cardboard front had been written in ink: [...]

"What d'you suppos [...] e General muttered. He wasn't asking a ques [...] to himself.

He flipped the notel [...] e entirely blank. He riffled the pages. Near th [...] age had been filled.

Ray got up and ben [...] l's shoulders, while Lambert looked over the [...]

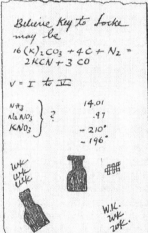

The characters and figures on the page were in the same thin, spidery hand as Keene's name on the cover. They appeared to be idle jottings, with a sprinkle of doodlings around the edges.

"Nothing," Lambert said with disgust.

The General said, "If it weren't for the e on the end of the word lock, I might agree. But that one letter…"

"That one letter makes it my name!" Ray cut in excitedly. "But what…"

"You've expressed it all very succinctly," the General said quietly.

"What!"

"Looks like he was drawing a picture of a milk bottle," Lambert commented.

"To me," the General admitted, "they look like hieroglyphics on a Babylonian cuspidor."

Ray frowned at the equation at the top of the page. "Wait a minute, sir," he said. "That formula—I saw it in the book I was studying last night. It's the reaction of nitrogen in a blast furnace to produce the small amount of cyanogen always present in blast furnace gases."

"Ah!" breathed the General. "Nitrogen."

"And that's what the figures represent," Ray went on. "He's put down the atomic weight and the melting and boiling points of nitrogen. The *V* stands for *valence.*"

"The milk bottle," said Lambert sourly, "must have been filled with rot-gut hooch!"

"Maybe he was thinking of a laboratory flask. No! I've got it. He was thinking of a blast furnace, and those doodlings are supposed to be the furnace."

"Now we know all about it," Lambert said with heavy sarcasm. "All we have to do is put the murderer under arrest."

"Nevertheless," the General said seriously, "this is an important find. What we want to learn now is how Keene's book got into the possession of this girl."

He went back and stood over the girl. Her eyelids twitched slightly.

"If we had some smelling salts," Ray began. "Maybe if I call the switchboard…"

The General was eyeing the prostrate form of Jackie North intently. "Wait!" he interrupted.

He drew a fresh cigar from his pocket, clipped the end and struck a match. When he had the Perfecto drawing he bent over the couch and, before Ray knew what he intended, had thrust the end under Jackie's nose. The smoke curled up directly into her nostrils.

Jackie coughed, almost strangling. Her eyes flew wide open.

"I thought that would bring you around," the General said. There was a gleam far back in his dark eyes. "Not too convincing an act, young lady."

Jackie said, "I—I don't feel well. I—I'm sick."

"Maybe," U. G. Flint said, "you simply don't want us to question you. It was a convenient time to faint. Is that it?"

Jackie sat up.

The General said, "I want you to tell us what you know about the murder at the laboratory last night."

"I don't know anything about it. I just heard about it this morning."

Ray helped the girl to her feet. She shook herself from his supporting arm, went over to her desk and sat down.

"It won't do," the General said. He held the blue notebook toward her. "I want you to tell me how you got this."

The girl's eyes flickered around the office quickly as if she were seeking a means of escape. "There's nothing to tell. I was at the laboratory last night. You know that. I found the notebook and picked it up. I intended to return it to Mr. Keene today."

"When did you find it?"

"Just after he"—she jerked her head toward Ray Locke—"just after he left."

"Tell us all about it," the General insisted remorselessly. "Where were you? How did you happen to find it? Where? Everything!"

Jackie North got up abruptly from her desk. For an instant Ray thought she was going to run out of the office. But she only walked over to the couch near Harris' desk and seated herself again.

This morning she was wearing powder blue. But the red silk scarf knotted loosely around her throat provided the exact shade to match her lips. She crossed her legs as she settled herself. Jackie North had pretty legs, rounded and graceful.

It occurred to Ray suddenly that he could never afford to have a secretary as pretty as Jackie North, not even if he personally owned the entire American-Consolidated Steel Company, because such a pretty secretary would definitely keep his mind away from business.

A secretary of his own. Ray wrenched his thoughts back to reality. He would be lucky if he had a *neck* of his own when everything was over.

"It was after Mr. Locke left," Jackie repeated. She seemed to be weighing each word with caution. "I left, too, but I came back again in about a quarter of an hour."

"Why did you go back?"

She met his hard eyes calmly. "Mr. Harris had asked me to go there last night."

"What for?"

"It was something confidential for him," she said. "I'd rather he told you about it."

"And I'd rather *you* told us." Lambert's voice was harsh.

The General cut in again. "We're going to talk with Harris," he said, quietly overruling the police detective. "We can find out from him at that time."

Once more Lambert looked angry. Once more he kept his mouth shut, but the muscles along his lean jaw knotted with the effort.

"Go on, Miss North," the General prompted.

"Everything was quiet," she said. "I thought I had the whole place to myself. Then I heard someone running down the steps from the chemical laboratory. I was in the big office and I went to look out into the corridor. It was Walter Keene. He looked very excited, and sort of…well, *grim*, you might say. He had some kind of an oblong yellow box with him and literally went dashing out of the building."

"Did he see you?"

She hesitated. "No. I was in the dark."

"What then?"

"Well, I went back to—to what I was doing. Then, after a little, I heard someone come in and go upstairs. I went out to look again."

"Whom did you see this time?"

"No one. I just heard the footsteps on the stairs. They were sort of slow and—and heavy like. When I got to the foot of the stairs, whoever it was had gone and I found this little notebook on the third step from the bottom. I decided it was Keene who had come back."

"And I think you were right," the General said grimly. "I think what you heard was the murderer carrying Keene's body upstairs. That's why the steps were slow and heavy. The notebook could have dropped from Keene's pocket while the killer was carrying him up."

The girl shuddered and her emotion appeared genuine. "How awful! If I'd known…"

"What did Cannon have to say about all this?" Flint demanded suddenly.

"Cannon?"

"Yes, Cannon. C-a-n-n-o-n."

"I don't know anyone named Cannon."

The General said, "Be careful now, Miss North. I'm warning you to tell the truth."

"I'm telling you the truth."

"And you don't know Glenn Cannon? How long have you been at Ironton, Miss North?"

"Nearly a year."

"Only a year?"

"Yes. I came here when Mr. Harris moved to Ironton.

The General's face cleared. "Oh, I see. You were his secretary when he was in New York. Harris brought you here with him?"

Jackie said, "No. I never worked for American-Consolidated Steel before I came here. I'd been with Youngstown Sheet and Tube and had good secretarial experience. When I heard of this opportunity through an employment service, I applied for the position."

The General regarded Jackie closely. "As secretary to the Assistant General Superintendent of such a large plant you have a very nice job."

"I like it," she agreed readily.

"And you want to keep it, I'm sure." The General spoke very quietly, but the implied threat did not escape the girl. "Now think carefully, Miss North. Are you sure you don't know Cannon? Didn't you ever hear his name mentioned?"

"Well..." Her eyes fell before the General's piercing scrutiny. "I didn't say I never heard the name mentioned."

The General pounced. "Who mentioned it?"

"This man"—she nodded again toward Ray—"was talking about Cannon last night."

"And that's the only time you've heard about him?" The General was relentless.

Jackie raised her eyes again. "No. I think I've heard either Mr. Tracy or Mr. Harris speak of him."

"Go on."

She seemed to reach a sudden decision. "All right," she said. "I *have* heard of Glenn Cannon before." She waved a small, slim hand toward the door to Tracy's office adjoining. "Sometimes when people talk unusually loudly in there, I can't help but overhear. I heard what happened when Cannon came in and applied for a job."

"When was this?"

"Two days ago. Just before Mr. Raymond Locke"—surprisingly there was venom in the way she pronounced Ray's name—"before Mr. Locke came in and was hired immediately over Mr. Harris' objection."

"Go ahead," the General prodded again as she paused.

"There was an angry argument. Both Cannon and Mr. Tracy were practically shouting. That's how I happened to hear. Tracy ordered Cannon out of the office. Tracy said Cannon had a 'hell of a nerve' to show his face around Ironton. He told him to get out and stay out and never to set foot inside his office again. After that..."

The door to the outside corridor opened and Harris came in. He started with surprised disapproval when he saw Ray, but to the latter's great relief, glanced past him to the other occupants of the room, and to all intents and purposes, ignored him.

"All through at the new furnace," he said to no one in particular. He bit the end from a cigar, spat the fragment of tobacco into the wastebasket. "She blew in nicely. Tracy's still in session with the Blast Furnace Super. He'll be in soon. He wants to see you, General."

U. G. Flint nodded. Then he turned again to Jackie North. "And after Tracy threw Cannon out?"

"He called Bixler on the telephone," she said. "He was still so mad he was yelling. He told Bixler that under no circumstances was Cannon to be allowed into the plant at any time."

"Anything else?"

"Isn't that enough?" Jackie seemed strangely excited by her own recital.

The General overlooked the disrespect of her last remark. "Bixler?" he said to Harris. "That's the big company guard we sent after Locke this morning?"

Harris said, "Yes. Bixler's chief of the company police force—a rough customer." He shifted the cigar to the other corner of his mouth and champed it between his teeth. "'Windpipe' Bixler, they call him, because he has a nice little habit, so I've been told, of getting his opponent by the throat, in a free-for-all. Bixler seems quite proud of his nickname."

"Perhaps," the General suggested, "*you* gave Cannon a pass into the plant?" He glanced at Harris inquiringly.

Harris said, "Not I. I think I remarked this morning that I'd never set eyes on the man. Anyhow, I wouldn't have countermanded Mr. Tracy's orders. In this case I agreed with him completely." He shot a meaningful glance at Ray.

"Then," the General said slowly, "how did Cannon get into the plant?" He flipped the switch on the intercommunication box. "I'd like to have you get hold of Bixler," he told Tracy's secretary. "Ask him if he's checked yet on whether any of his men let Cannon into the plant last night. If he says no, make sure he's checked each entrance gate. When you have his reply, let me know."

Lieutenant Lambert leaned forward in his chair. His forefinger stabbed at Quentin Harris. "Assuming that Locke was not just lying and that he actually did see Cannon around the laboratory last night, what do *you* think your secretary was doing there with him?"

Jackie North said, "I told you no one was with me."

"Quiet, sister. I'm talking to your boss now."

Harris said, "I wouldn't know. Undoubtedly Locke is lying."

"That's what I think," Lambert agreed. "But I don't know why, on a thing that's not very important." He turned back to Jackie. "Now, sister, time's come for you to tell us what *you* were doing over there."

Jackie said simply, "I've already said that Mr. Harris asked me to go there."

"How about it, Mr. Harris? Why did you ask her to go into the plant in the middle of the night?"

Quentin Harris eyes met those of U. G. Flint momentarily. Then, "I'm sure there would have been no reason for me to do such a thing!" he said coolly.

There was sudden panic in Jackie North's big brown eyes. "But, Mr. Harris," she cried, "you can't say a thing like that. They'll think I had something to do with that…with the *murder!*"

The voice of Tracy's secretary cut in suddenly from the desk box. "I've talked with Bixler, sir. He says none of his men let Cannon into the plant last night. None of them even saw Cannon."

"He's been in touch with each entrance to the works?"

"Yes, sir. That's what he says."

Lieutenant Lambert was sitting tensely on his chair edge. "Someone's lying," he said belligerently. "I want to know why this girl went into the plant last night. Now look, Mr. Harris—"

The General interrupted. "The testimony doesn't altogether jibe, that's a fact. But these details aren't too important. We'll get to the bottom of it all, later."

"What's the matter with doing it right now?" Lambert demanded. He swung savagely to Quentin Harris.

"Incidentally," he said, chopping his words with brutal emphasis, "we've been told that *you* made some remarks about how Keene needed to be killed. What about that, Harris?"

Harris was startled. "Who said that?"

"I ask 'em, you answer 'em," Lambert snapped.

Harris' teeth almost bit his cigar in two. "I don't like your attitude," he told the police officer curtly. "Anyone would think I'm the one under suspicion for killing Keene."

Lambert didn't mince words. "You *are*! Everyone within a hundred miles of this plant is suspect until we nab the killer. No reason why a big shot couldn't have done the job as well as a little fellow. Just because a guy's got a big job doesn't mean he's out of the picture."

There was ruddy color in Harris' beefy face. "You're absurd!" he spluttered. "Why should I want to kill a plant employee? Why, Keene was no more than a skilled workman, a technician. What good would it do me to murder such a man?"

"I don't know," Lambert admitted bitterly. "But, by God, I'm going to find out!"

The General sat very straight in his chair, his face absolutely devoid of expression. "It was my understanding you were going to let me conduct this investigation," he said coldly. "If that's the case, I should appreciate being allowed to do so in my own way."

"It was *my* understanding," Lambert repeated the words angrily, "that you were attempting to find out who killed this guy Keene!"

The General stood up abruptly. "I suggest we adjourn to Mr. Tracy's office." He bowed stiffly to Jackie North. "Thank you, Miss North, for your information. At the moment I think we needn't bother you any further."

SEVEN

Not until they were settled again in Tracy's office did the General reply to Lieutenant Lambert's remark.

"What else," he asked icily, "do you think I've been trying to do if it isn't to find Keene's slayer?"

Lambert returned the General's stare without flinching. "It almost seems," he said bluntly, "as if you're trying to *avoid* information, trying to whitewash the most likely suspects. For instance Locke here, then the North girl, and now Harris."

The General's bald streak glowed suddenly pink. His fathomless eyes gleamed excitedly.

"Lambert," he roared, "I've handled matters as far beyond your depth as the Tuscorora Deep would be over the head of a pearl diver!"

"Just the same," Lambert insisted stubbornly, "you're not being very skillful about this. The police would…"

U. G. Flint's rage subsided as suddenly as it had started. "You have the authority of the police department behind you," he told Lambert evenly. "If you want to take matters out of my hands, you can. And this is the time to do it. Let's just get it settled right now, once and for all. If you wish me to bow out, let me know so I can inform New York immediately."

"Handle it your own way," Lambert muttered sullenly. He sunk back into the chair depths.

The General said, "That's better. Now, just for your information, I might say that the answers to the particular questions you have raised are a splendid demonstration of mind over matter." His eyes twinkled momentarily. "I don't mind if they are not answered, because they do not matter."

Lambert did not reply, but his expression showed his disgust.

The General turned to Quentin Harris as if there had been no interruption. "Can you tell us anything at all," he asked, "which might be helpful on this murder angle?"

"First I knew about it," Harris said, "was when the laboratory called this morning. You were in my office at the time, General. We got Mr.

Tracy, informed him of what had happened, and the three of us went over together."

"You didn't happen to be around the plant last night yourself?"

"Not in the plant. I was in this building working in my office until very late. I didn't leave until nearly three in the morning."

"But you didn't go inside the works?"

"No."

The anteroom door opened and in came Leonard Tracy. U. G. Flint made a move as if to get up and give Tracy the desk chair.

Tracy said, "Stay where you are, General." He slid into a seat against the wall.

"We've been discussing the murder," Flint informed him. "And we've developed some very pertinent and interesting facts."

"Glad to hear it," Lieutenant Lambert muttered sulkily. "I'd thought there was no progress at all."

U. G. Flint swung around briskly to the police officer. "For your information," he said, "young Locke has helped find the weapon which killed Keene. That, you will agree, is progress. And since Ray Locke was instrumental in leading us to the actual scene of the murder, I thought it only fitting he should sit in with us while we talked with the other persons involved."

Lambert perked up visibly. "You located the murder weapon? Why didn't you tell me?"

"I'm telling you now." The General brought Lambert up to date on their visit to the hammer shop and discovery of the swage. "I took the precaution of carrying it over to the laboratory building, and locking it in a closet off Ashley's office. Here's the key."

The homicide lieutenant got up quickly. "I want to get my men busy on that right away. There might be prints."

"Just what I was going to suggest," Flint said. "Also that you have your men check the time cards of all the people we've interviewed this morning to verify what they've said."

Lambert looked hard at Quentin Harris. "Shall I check his time card, also?"

Harris' face got red again. "It happens that I don't punch any time card. I'm Assistant General Superintendent of this plant. Everyone up to that rank is required to punch. I'm not."

"Excuse *me!*" Lambert's inflection was sarcastic.

After the lieutenant had gone, U. G. Flint turned to Tracy. "I think it would be an excellent idea," he said, nodding toward Ray Locke, "if this young man could be transferred to the Test Department instead of wasting his very obvious talents as an ordinary workman."

"I'd thought of that myself, General," Tracy said quickly. "It occurred to me, however, if that were done, we at this plant might be subject to criticism from the higher-ups in New York. After that unfortunate episode—"

Flint interrupted. "Yes, I know. And I can well understand your reluctance to place yourself in a situation which might be misunderstood. I shall make sure personally that no such misapprehension occurs."

Ray glanced at Quentin Harris. He expected the blocky Assistant General Superintendent to make some objection, as he had before. To Ray's surprise, Harris kept his mouth shut.

Tracy said, "You will explain that this change is being made at your own specific request, General?"

U. G. Flint said, "That's right. Is it all arranged, then?"

Tracy nodded. "It's all arranged!"

He gave Ray a friendly smile. From where the latter was sitting, the ugly red scar of the man's burn was not visible and Tracy looked more handsome than ever before.

"Well, General," he said, after a pause, "I suppose you've sewed up the case against our Ironton killer."

U. G. Flint laughed mirthlessly. "It isn't quite that simple. I'm afraid there are still some devious paths to be explored before we can put our finger on the guilty party."

"With your ability, General," Tracy said smoothly, "the final result is inevitable. The murderer might as well confess right now."

"You flatter me!" U. G. Flint settled back, jiggling comfortably in Tracy's desk chair. "We already have five people who had both the possible opportunity and the possible motive, and another with at least a motive. Probably there are more."

"Who are the five?" Tracy inquired.

"Locke, Gaylord, Miss Dunne, Miss North and Cannon." The General ticked them off on his fingers. "No one except Locke saw Cannon. Locke might have been mistaken. But the rest were definitely near the laboratory building last night."

"Who's the other?" Tracy asked.

"'Windpipe' Bixler," Flint said. He went on to tell Tracy what Gaylord had said. "I've already asked Lieutenant Lambert to find out where Bixler was last night. Of course, Bixler's motive seems very weak for murder, but a man of Bixler's type might think as little of killing as you or I would of hitting another man with our fist."

"An ugly customer," Harris agreed.

"In fact, *all* the motivations seem weak," the General went on reflectively, "at least the *surface* motivations. Now if it were Ashley who had been killed that would be different. Promotion for either Gaylord or Miss Dunne would be involved."

"Ben Gaylord would be next in line," Tracy murmured.

"But Ashley wasn't the one murdered. Therefore, ambition as the motive appears to be ruled out." The General fixed Tracy with a speculative eye. "It leads to the thought that Keene might have been killed as a protective measure."

"Protective?"

"Yes. By some Test Department employee, say, who was involved with him in this trouble we've been having on falsified tests."

"You think Keene was mixed up in that?" Tracy exhibited the greatest interest.

"I *know* it." Ray wondered at the big man's emphasis. How could he be so sure of a thing like that?

But Tracy did not question the General's statement.

"Keene was only a pawn in the game," the General went on. "He was involved only to the extent of doctoring specified chemical analyses when requested to do so. Someone other than Keene in the department provided the brains. Someone who knows steel from A to Izzard." The General shot a significant glance at Ray. "Someone smart enough to fool experienced outside inspectors."

"You mean either Ashley or Gaylord, then." Tracy spoke confidently. "Ashley is a metallurgical engineer. He has written monographs on the crystalline structures of iron and steel. Ben Gaylord came up through the ranks from a plate mill gauger. Both men know the inspection game backward and forward."

"Looks as though we can count Ashley out. Apparently he was not in the plant last night. Has an alibi not only for the time of Keene's death, but for the entire evening."

"Then you've narrowed it down to Gaylord!"

The General laughed. "Not quite that fast. All the others I mentioned are still in the picture. Anyhow, both Gaylord and Miss Dunne were in the plant just on the edge of the time set by the Medical Examiner. The difference of half an hour, and the time of Keene's death probably isn't exact to within a full hour, would let them both out, too—that is, provided their time cards check with the stories they've told us."

A wry smile spread over Tracy's handsome face. "Time cards wouldn't mean much when a murder alibi is involved," he said. "It's always possible to have someone else punch the clock for you. It's been done before, in every large plant."

"Exactly."

"I'm particularly interested," Tracy said, "in the matter of Cannon. What did you find out about that?"

"We haven't made any progress on that angle yet," Flint said. "Bixler has checked and says positively Cannon was not admitted through any of the plant gates last night."

"Then he wasn't there," Tracy said almost as if he were relieved. "You saw someone else, Ray—someone who resembled Cannon."

Ray said, "That's been suggested. Could be, of course. But I'm satisfied in my own mind I saw Glenn himself."

The General trimmed a fresh cigar, accepting with a curt nod the book of matches Ray held out to him, then glanced thoughtfully at the large "L" printed on the cover.

"A relic of former days," Ray volunteered. "Found them when I went through Dad's things. Not much else was left."

The General nodded understandingly, returned the matches to Ray, and continued as if there had been no interruption.

"The real motive for Keene's murder might be something entirely personal. It might be based upon relationship, or revenge, or…well, a thousand and one things. It could be entirely trivial."

He rocked serenely in Tracy's chair. "I've seen men kill each other over a lousy dollar. That's why I say that motives can be trivial to the point of absurdity. And it's why we can't count out Bixler, or any of the others."

Tracy smiled broadly. "Even Quentin Harris might have killed him. Or maybe you did it yourself, General."

"I'm still a young man!" the General remarked. "I look forty-five or older, but I'm still in my thirties. And my life is more than half over. I had a hard time when I was a youngster!" He stopped rocking and sat up suddenly straight in the chair. "I'm quite capable of killing a man like Keene—quite capable. Or maybe you did it yourself, Tracy. As administrative head of these mills you would have one of the best motives of all. Particularly if you'd happened to know that Keene had been helping fake some of the tests, or if you were mixed up in it personally in any way. After all, you have an important and lucrative position to protect."

Tracy smiled, but it seemed a bit forced. *"Touché!"* he said.

The General said, "Locke, I don't think we'll need you now for a while. Keep your eyes open in your new job at the laboratory. If you run into anything you think I should know about, call me immediately—day or night. I'm staying at the George Washington. And… I'll be talking with you again, soon."

Ray went through Tracy's anteroom and along the side corridor past the door of Harris' office. Jackie North was at her desk, typing as usual. Ray stuck his head around the door jamb.

"Miss North," he said, "may I speak with you a moment?"

She glanced at him without interest. "I'm busy," she said and went on with her work.

"I could have put you on a spot," he insisted. "You lied about Glenn Cannon. But I kept my mouth shut. I don't know why I should protect you."

She got up and came over to the door. "Please go away," she said in a low tone. "You're going to get us both into trouble."

"You're in trouble already," Ray said. "You practically accused your boss of being a liar. If he doesn't fire you something's rotten."

"You don't know what you're talking about. Go away!"

He planted himself solidly in the doorway. "It's *my* neck that's at stake in this affair. I don't know why Flint didn't force you to explain, but I want to know why you lied about not knowing Cannon."

"I don't know him."

Ray said, "When I met you at the lab last night you called Cannon by his first name."

"You're mistaken," she said. But suddenly she put her small hand on his arm and pushed him outside into the hall, following. "We might be overheard in there."

"Okay by me," he said bluntly. "I have nothing to conceal. But I'm asking you again: if you didn't know Cannon, how did it happen you used his first name?"

She gave him a scorching look. "You're imagining things that didn't happen."

"My imagination isn't that good," Ray said quietly. "I asked you how come Cannon was back at Ironton. You said he wasn't back. And you added then what you told Flint this morning, that Mr. Tracy had practically thrown *Glenn* out of his office. You called him *Glenn*—not Cannon. I remember distinctly."

"Maybe," she suggested, "you should see a psychiatrist. You're suffering from hallucinations."

"You said," Ray went on, ignoring her sarcasm, "that I must have some kind of a pull to get a job at Ironton—a pull with Mr. Tracy that Glenn Cannon didn't have."

"Haven't you?"

"Why was it necessary to drag Mr. Tracy into it?" Ray demanded severely. "Mr. Tracy is a fine man. If he threw Cannon out of his office he must have had good and sufficient reason."

"Why did he hire *you* then?"

"I was never an employee of the steel company," Ray said. "Mr. Tracy has to think how it would seem to the high officials in New York if he hired back a former employee convicted of dishonesty. That didn't apply in my case."

"From what I heard," Jackie observed pointedly, "you were in the same mess with Cannon…up to your neck!"

"I was framed," Ray told her earnestly. "I had nothing whatever to do with accepting that worthless steel."

"So you've said! Well, mightn't Cannon have been framed, too?"

"It could be," Ray admitted slowly. "But if I were you, I'd steer clear of the guy, Miss North. The fact that Mr. Tracy wouldn't hire him back shows in itself—"

"The great Tracy can do no wrong, is that it? You're very quick to stick up for Leonard Tracy, aren't you?"

"He's been a friend to me."

"Has he?" she asked scornfully. "That's what you think! And it makes you just about the biggest sucker I've ever seen."

"Why do you say that?"

Unexpectedly her attitude changed. She took his hand in hers. Her fingers were warm and friendly. "What you need," she said, "is someone to look after you! You're just a kid after all."

Ray was startled. He didn't like to have a pretty girl his own age accuse him of being a kid. But before he could express his outrage, Jackie was speaking again.

"You *did* think you were helping me," she admitted. "The least I can do, then, is to warn you. I'd hate to have you killed when I might prevent it."

"Killed!"

"Yes. You'll surely be killed if someone doesn't open your eyes to what it's all about. You think Tracy is your friend. Actually, he's your worst enemy."

Ray said, "Why, that's perfectly ridiculous. He gave me a job and…"

Jackie said, "Hush! Listen to me." She plucked the red-framed glasses from her slightly retrouseé little nose. Golden specks in her soft brown eyes glinted with excitement. "I heard something else that went on in Tracy's office, something I haven't mentioned to anyone…yet." Her voice dropped. "Yesterday morning, just after Tracy had told Harris to arrange to put you on the payroll, I started into Tracy's office to ask him about something Harris wanted. I got the door partly open and heard Tracy talking on the telephone. He didn't see me. I backed out and shut the door softly so he never knew I'd overheard him."

She was whispering now, so low that Ray had to bend close to hear. He could smell the faint scent of her hair and the perfume she was wearing. It made him feel he'd like to go on protecting Jackie North indefinitely.

"Tracy was talking to Bixler," she said. "There was no shouting this time. Tracy was telling Bixler he'd hired you. Then he said to Bixler that no matter how carefully a steel plant is run, accidents can happen. He said that there was always a possibility something might happen to *you*. You might slip and fall into a ladle full of molten steel. Or a crane operator might drop a load of plates while you were walking underneath."

Jackie stopped then, her eyes fastened on Ray's face. "Don't you believe me?"

He said, "Sure. I believe you. But what of it? Mr. Tracy was right. Accidents do happen in steel mills. We all know that."

"I think he *wanted* you to he killed!"

"Why, that doesn't make sense! Why should Mr. Tracy want anything to happen to me?"

"I don't know," she said. She jerked her hand away from him suddenly. "You figure it out. I've warned you now. I've told you what he said. And the way he said it, he was practically ordering Bixler to make sure something did happen to you!"

EIGHT

Ray Locke went back to his room in the bleak, malodorous rooming house. He changed from his work clothes to the good suit he had worn upon his arrival at Ironton, then took the street car into the city.

Only a few cents remained in his pockets. His first stop was a pawn shop, where he left his platinum-banded wrist watch. Emerging with folding money in his possession once more, he headed for the main office of the telephone company.

When he left there, twenty minutes later, he had definite information to show that his own statement to the authorities was not based upon an impossibility. Glenn Cannon had been released from prison at about the same time as Ray himself. The officials at the penitentiary had no information as to where Cannon might have gone after his parole.

From the telephone building, Rays next call was the public library, a huge structure, its gray masonry now a sooty black from years of exposure to smoke from the mills.

In the high-vaulted, central reading room, Ray went up to the Inquiry desk. "I'm looking for Miss Jackson," he informed the wrinkled little old lady on duty there.

"I'm Miss Jackson."

Ray said, "Fine. My boss, Mr. Ashley, asked me to see you. He thinks he must have left a page of notes in a book he was reading here last night."

"Mr. Ashley?" She patted a lock of yellowish-white hair into place. Then comprehension dawned in her washed-out blue eyes. "Oh, you mean Mr. Christopher Ashley of the steel company."

Ray nodded. "That's right. The book is Masey's *Micrographic Analysis of Austenitic Steels.*"

"You must have the title confused," she informed him kindly. "Masey's book is reserved." She pointed to a glass-enclosed bookcase behind the desk. "It's been under lock and key for forty-eight hours. We're holding it for Professor Quine of the mining engineering staff at Tech. No one would have been allowed to take it last evening, even to read in the library."

Ray contrived to look bewildered. "That's mighty queer. I could have sworn that was the book he mentioned." He started to turn away, then swung back to the librarian. "Don't you recall seeing Mr. Ashley last night?"

"No," she said positively, "I don't. But I was in and out of the stacks a great deal and could easily have missed him, though he generally comes and speaks to me."

"Well, thanks anyway," he said. "Evidently I've got the whole thing mixed up."

Ray worried about this conflicting scrap of information all the way back to the mill. He knew he did not need to report at the laboratory until eight the next morning, but he mingled with the stream of workers on the midnight shift and pretended to punch back into the plant.

There were lights on the second floor of the test lab and a hundred-watt bulb in the gooseneck over the side entrance near Ashley's office glared harshly. Ray veered away from the blue glow of the machine shop windows to approach through the shadows.

He had almost reached the building when he saw a light glimmer fleetingly downstairs in the office section. It was a stealthy light which vanished almost immediately. Ray stopped, stepping closer to the brick wall.

In a moment the light gleamed again. Evidently someone with a flashlight was roaming the offices.

The third time the light showed, it was through the window next to Ashley's office. Ray dodged around the corner beyond the glare from the gooseneck bulb, easing to the side of the pane from which the beam came. It shone steadily now.

He investigated cautiously with one eye at the edge of the sash. He was looking into the Test Department's clerical office. The flashlight had been set on a desk top so that its beam shone along the crowded row of filing cabinets.

A man was standing with his back toward Ray, rooting through an open file drawer. He pulled out some old test sheets, brought them over nearer the light to examine them more closely, then shoved them into a leather briefcase on the desk behind the flashlight. He turned then, and Ray could see his face.

The man was Quentin Harris.

Ray didn't linger after that. He slid away from the window, went on swiftly around the building and on out of the plant.

His first morning on the new job next day was uneventful. Ashley was not around. Gaylord seemed pleased to have Ray working with him. The Chief Inspector put him to work on the big Norton testing machine, pulling tests for tensile strength.

It was like old times. Ray forgot his uneasiness while he was so busy. But his dice, when he consulted them at odd moments throughout the morning, had developed a strange reluctance to show anything except twos and threes.

The jaws of the trap became clearly visible to him for the first time during lunch hour, when he decided to relax and stretch his legs with a short walk around the plant. He recalled Jackie North's warning but in daylight her fears seemed remote and unreal.

He went into the rail mill, standing for a few minutes to watch white-hot, oblong billets slide endlessly through the tiers, or stands, of rolls. The billets emerged from the furnaces upon moving trains of small rollers. They passed through the huge rolls themselves, moved back and forth as the driving gears, line upon line of massive metal cogwheels black with grease, reversed continually. Each pass beneath the rolls narrowed and lengthened the billet, shaping it, until it finally emerged in a long ribbon of steel rail to be cut into proper lengths by hot-saws at the far end of the mill.

Fascinated as always by the sight, Ray went out on a narrow footway which crossed the moving beds upon which the glowing steel shuttled back and forth. He stood on the catwalk, arms against the small pipe guard rail, engrossed with the chaos of roaring machinery, the clang of metal and the shrill repeated blasts of whistle signals.

Suddenly he was half lifted and violently shoved. It was so entirely unexpected that Ray plunged head first over the narrow railing before he knew what was happening. Only the instinctive clutch of his fingers at the pipe guard rail saved him. They caught, held him, as waves of heat struck upward from a white-hot rail section sliding past underneath the catwalk.

Ray struggled back through the space below the guard rail. A hulking form in a blue uniform was on the footway beside him. Bixler's battered features wore an expression of exaggerated dismay, his protruding jaw sagged.

"You want to watch yourself, bud!" he said. "Might get hurt stumblin' around thataway."

"You dirty bastard! You tried to push me into the rolls!" Ray accused.

He was trembling in spite of himself. The fate he had so narrowly escaped was a dreadful one. Had he landed on the moving bed below, Ray knew he would have gone through the rolls before the boss roller could have had time to stop his gears.

He had once heard of a man to whom that had happened. The poor devil had first been crushed into the shape of a rail, bones pulverized. Then, terrific heat had bloated the corpse into a long, hideous balloon, ghastly beyond imagination.

Bixler's phony apprehension gave place to a scowl. "Don't be givin' out loose talk," be advised. "You're drunk maybe, fella. We don't like guys to be drinkin' on company time!"

Red rage was stiffening Ray's shaky nerves. "You can't get away with it, Bixler," he said. "I think you're the man who tried to drop a chunk of steel on me at the Open Hearth day before yesterday. What's the big idea?"

Bixler's massive jaw thrust out belligerently. "The idea is this, bud: *you ain't wanted around this here steel works!* If you got any sense at all you'll git out. Git out an' stay out!"

Ray stood as if rooted while he watched Bixler disappear into the yard beyond the rail mill. His mind was whirling confusion. Jackie North must be right, after all. But it simply didn't make sense.

As he walked back slowly to the testing lab, Ray was thinking of Leonard Tracy and of his father, Belden Locke. The two men had been business friends for many years. Just before the wreck which brought death to his father, Ray believed there had even been some kind of business venture in which his father and Tracy were jointly engaged, but he knew nothing of the details.

About his father's finances, Ray knew little except that there had always seemed to be plenty of money.

However, when he had been released from prison, Ray found little remaining of his father's estate. Belden Locke's bank accounts had been closed out only a few months before the wreck of the *Comet*. The cash had gone, apparently, over the counter in personal drafts to Ray's father. In addition, Ray had found statements from various brokerage firms, revealing that Belden Locke's securities had been turned into cash, as well. But the cash was gone.

Ray hadn't the faintest idea what his father had done with the money. It was just one more inexplicable item in a jumble which overwhelmed him with its seeming hopelessness.

He punched out of the plant at quitting time, grabbed a bite to eat, and came back along the dingy Ironton street past the steel company's Administration Building. It was not yet dark, but the lamps were on in Tracy's office and Ray could see the dapper executive through the window, seated at his circular desk, busy with papers.

Ray walked along the street slowly, turned and came back past Tracy's window. He kept that up for more than an hour. Finally, as he loitered outside the executive office, peering in at Tracy, a stentorian bellow came from the plant entrance gate Number One a short distance away.

"Hey, you!"

Ray turned. One of the uniformed plant police was walking toward him.

"I been watching you," the man said. "You been hanging around too long. Now go on, beat it! Don't let me see you around here again tonight."

Ray didn't argue. He swung on his heel, crossed the street. He passed long rows of dingy, unpainted frame buildings, every third one a bar-room. For two blocks he felt the suspicious eyes of the plant guard on his back.

Half a dozen blocks away was another entrance to the Ironton Works. Ray crossed the street again, went to the gate house, took a card at random from those on the board beside the timekeeper's window. He held it near the time clock, pressed down on the lever. The bell rang.

Ray put the unstamped card back onto the rack. The gateman took a cursory glance at Ray's identification badge as he went on into the plant.

The building nearest the executive offices was a small two-story structure, headquarters for the plant's narrow-gauge railroad system. Offices were upstairs; the bottom portion of the building was divided into locker rooms with washing facilities for the workmen.

Ray stood just inside the locker room door where he could see the Administration Building. His chances of accomplishing anything this evening were very slim. He was quite aware of that. Tracy might have left the office already, while Ray was making the circuitous trip to avoid the cop at Number One Gate. Most likely, when Tracy did leave, he would simply get his car from the parking space behind the offices and drive away. While a man like Tracy would not count his working hours, still he did not work *all* the time.

Daylight faded rapidly now. Lights blossomed in the windows of the dreary buildings beyond the high fence surrounding the steel works. Ray waited patiently.

Nearly an hour later, when he was just about to give up in disgust, a tall, slender figure emerged from the side door of the Administration Building and headed for Gate Number One. An overhead light gave Ray a fleeting glimpse of Tracy's handsome, regular features.

The General Superintendent cut across the open from the entrance gate, turned his back to the blast furnaces and strode rapidly in the direction of the Bessemer and the soaking pits. Keeping a safe distance behind, Ray followed.

A string of tipping ladles on buggies drawn by a diminutive plant locomotive cast white radiance like the noonday sun as they spilled their contents into the hot metal mixer three hundred yards from the converter mill. Ray ducked out of Tracy's line of vision behind the hulking steel shell of the first two-hundred-ton mixer.

But Tracy did not look back. He went on past the converter building, past the long gray structure housing the soaking pits. Ray could see then that he was headed straight for the Open Hearth.

But the General Superintendent did not turn into Quirk's shack-like office at the end of the Open Hearth. Instead, he rounded the corner of the thousand-foot building, going along the blank side below the charging floor of the furnaces.

There were few entrances into the Open Hearth plant from that side. No workmen were in the open space between the building and the inlet which was Ironton's boundary. Ray knew if he attempted to dog Tracy's footsteps into that long open stretch he would be as conspicuous as a foundry molder in overalls at a convention of steel mill executives.

He ducked quickly into the entrance near Quirk's cubbyhole, ran up an iron stairway to a wide floor built of steel plates. This was the charging floor of the Open Hearth, the side of the furnaces from which they were fed their enormous rations of pig iron, steel scrap, ore and other ingredients.

As Ray came up, a "Low-type" charging machine was rolling like a juggernaut two hundred feet to his right, its massive bulk spanning rails twenty feet apart. The building wall beyond the furnace doors was broken at intervals with embrasure-like windows called ports. Ray darted quickly to the nearest and peered out. Below him and a hundred feet ahead, he could see Leonard Tracy's shadowy form plowing steadily forward as light from the ports above him spilled down.

Ray moved swiftly past piles of dolomite, scrap and fluorspar. The charging machine had stopped. It thrust out a massive arm, seized an oblong, cast-iron box, or buggy, on narrow gauge tracks beside Number Four furnace. The open door of the furnace winked like a white-hot eye as a man with blue glasses shouted orders. The box rotated, dumping its contents into the flaming interior.

A quarter way along the building, Ray caught up with Tracy and paralleled the man's course directly above him. No one on the charging floor paid the least attention to Ray. Everyone was too busy.

Checking on Tracy through the ports, Ray went clear on to the end of the Open Hearth building. He was beginning to wonder if the General Superintendent intended to visit some other part of the plant. Then Tracy finally stopped, just short of the end furnace.

Ray watched from above, ready to duck back out of sight if Tracy should happen to glance up. He saw the General Superintendent fumbling with something at the side of the building. Then suddenly Tracy stepped forward and disappeared. There was no entrance visible at this point. Ray was puzzled as to where the man had gone.

Quickly he crossed the charging floor to the alley between Number Eleven and Number Twelve furnaces. He came out on the platform behind Number Eleven, twenty feet above cinder pit level. Perhaps, he thought, Tracy had gone through some opening which led directly between the furnaces to the pouring floor or cinder pit of the plant.

But there was no sign of the General Superintendent. Number Twelve furnace, to Ray's left as he looked out over the pouring floor, was cold. From the looks of the rust and cinder incrustations on its buck-stays and tie rods, Ray judged it had not been in active operation for some time. Number Eleven, however, was working into the period of its lime boil. Ray could hear flaming gases hiss through its ports above its molten bath of metal.

Back in the direction from which Ray had followed Tracy, one of the furnaces was in process of being tapped. A thick stream of glowing metal was pouring through a spout into a fifteen-foot teeming ladle, filling that whole portion of the plant with blinding brilliance.

Ray ducked back to the window on the charging floor. Tracy had still not reappeared. Ray hesitated momentarily. Then he went down the iron stairs at the very end of the building, cut around the corner outside and approached the spot where Tracy had vanished. He moved gingerly, ready to duck instantly if Tracy should reappear.

He found an iron door set in the masonry. The padlock which had secured it was open, hanging in the staple. Ray thought he could hear faint sounds of someone moving around just inside the door.

Hastily he retreated again to the vantage point of the port above. Twenty minutes later Leonard Tracy reappeared. Ray heard the *snick* of the padlock as the General Superintendent snapped it shut. He waited until Tracy had been gone five minutes, then he picked up a sledge from the side of Number Eleven furnace and went back down.

He broke the padlock with one good blow of the sledge. The iron door led into the checker-work chambers beneath the charging floor in front of the inactive Number Twelve furnace. A tunnel-like arch of masonry loomed blackly in front of Ray.

He fumbled in his pockets, found a paper book of matches. It was the second time today his father's matches had come in handy. Only one match remained. Ray struck it and then, forgetting that the match book had his initial printed on the cover, he cast it aside.

The spurting flame showed him the last thing he had expected to find—an electric switch. The regenerative chambers had been wired for lighting.

He flipped the switch. He was in the gas chamber, thirty-one feet long, eight wide and some eighteen feet from the firebrick floor to the extremity of the roof arch. When an open hearth furnace is in operation, the gas chamber, as well as the air chamber which extends beside it separated by a firebrick wall, is crossed and recrossed by white walls and layers of firebrick tile which form a checker-work grid for the purpose of storing heat from the products of combustion and imparting it to cold gas and air entering the furnace. This chamber where Ray found himself had been dismantled, ripped free of its checker-work.

What had once been a roaring inferno of flame and glowing masonry, was now nothing more than a long brick room. When Ray investigated, he found openings cut through the masonry to connect with the adjoining air chamber and the maze of flues and ports which had been the furnace regenerators.

There were other things in the former checker-work chambers which interested Ray, too: the bench, like those in the Test Department's chemical laboratory, which stood at the far end of the room, nearest the inactive furnace; the firebrick-lined circular opening in the wall extending in the direction of Number Eleven furnace next door; the cast iron wheel, like that of a large valve, embedded in the masonry wall just above and to the side of the flue-like opening.

Experimentally, Ray gave the wheel a half turn. The first result was a hissing noise, then suddenly a bright cylinder of fire lanced through the wall opening with a roar like the flame from a blow-torch. The flue connected, evidently, with the actively operating checker-work beneath Number Eleven furnace, adjoining. Ray hastily twisted the valve shut again.

He glanced over all the apparatus on the laboratory bench. There were queer arrangements of glass and metal tubing, with heavy iron fittings seemingly designed to connect with the flue through which the flame had come. Ray could not determine their purpose. He noted that not only was the room wired for lighting, but heavy cables and a transformer indicated that considerable current was available for the many coils, rheostats and other electrical equipment also arranged along the work bench.

In the air chamber connecting, Ray found an ordinary office desk. There were papers on the desk which he flipped through rapidly. There was nothing which meant very much to him. Notes on various plans for fixation of atmospheric nitrogen were followed by those on the old Birkeland-Eyde process, the cyanamide process discovered by Frank and Caro, and on the modern Haber process. There were also detailed layouts of the fixation plants at Notodden and at Rjukan in Norway.

If Ray's eyes had not been sharp, his senses stimulated by discovery of the checker-work laboratory, he would certainly have missed his last and most interesting find of all. He was actually turning to leave when a point of light from the brickwork at the top of the air chamber caught his attention.

The luminous spot was a reflection of the electric bulb from a polished metal surface. Ray reached it by putting the desk chair on top of the desk and then climbing up.

Stuck up into one of the fanlike flues leading to the inactive furnace above, a brass box had been pushed almost entirely out of sight.

It was a heavy box, with a complicated and elaborate design of Chinese dragons worked into the yellow metal. The box had been battered, twisted out of shape as if by repeated blows with a sledge. The intricate puzzle lock which had once secured the contents was shattered beyond repair.

The box lid also had been split into three segments. Ray pulled them aside. The inside of the box was bare, completely devoid of secrets.

Suddenly Ray remembered the brass fragment he had picked from the dirt floor of the forge shop. He fished it from his pocket.

The delicate lines he had previously noticed without understanding formed part of a dragon's tail, coiling around the box.

The bit of metal fitted precisely into the broken corner.

NINE

Three-quarters of an hour later, acutely conscious of his stained work clothes, Ray came through the swank lobby of the George Washington Hotel and was whisked upward in a red plush elevator to the seventeenth floor.

The General met him at the door of Suite 17-D. He seemed even more immaculate than before in the dinner clothes he was now wearing. A contrast in black and white, his starched white shirtfront pointed up the blackness of his hair and mustache.

He waved Ray to a seat on a yellow leather lounge in the large, pleasant sitting room.

"Cigar?" he offered, passing a full box.

Ray shook his head. "Thanks, but I don't use them."

"Useless habit," the General agreed. He selected one for himself, then stretched comfortably in a yellow brocaded chair with his feet propped on the matching ottoman. He seemed in a most expansive mood.

"You asked me," Ray began tentatively, "to report anything new around Ironton."

"I meant exactly what I said."

"Well, I've had several experiences since yesterday," Ray admitted. "It'll quite likely cost me my job if I tell you about them."

"It's more likely to cost you your neck if you don't," the General reminded Ray conversationally.

"Very true, truer in fact than you realize. It almost cost me my neck this morning."

The General looked up sharply, quickened interest in his strong, deep voice. "So? Tell me about it, Locke." Ray told of his encounter with Bixler on the rail mill catwalk and of his narrow escape from a particularly gruesome death.

U. G. Flint studied Ray thoughtfully. "This is an entirely unexpected angle, Locke. What dealings have you had with this man Bixler prior to your present employment at Ironton?"

"None at all, sir. I never heard of Bixler until he brought me with him to the lab yesterday morning."

"Hmmm. The man must have had some reason for his action—unless he's a psychopathic case."

Ray said, "I have an idea about the reason, but that's what puts me up a tree. I'm likely either to lose my job or make you think I'm an idiot. In addition, there's the probability that I'm acting in a disloyal manner toward someone who's been my friend."

A curious gleam shone deep in the General's eyes. "Come on, Locke," he said impatiently. "Stop beating around the bush! Do I have to swear to an affidavit that I intend to protect your confidence? Isn't the fact that I arranged with the Open Hearth people to confirm your excuse for being at the laboratory the night of Keene's death sufficient proof of my sincerity?"

So it was the General who had been responsible for sidetracking Lambert and the police! Ray felt suddenly ashamed of his hesitation at confiding in the man. Yet he couldn't avoid the feeling that he might be acting unfairly toward Leonard Tracy.

"I was warned yesterday," he said slowly, "that Mr. Tracy had instructed Bixler to see to it that I met with an accident around the plant."

"Tracy?" The General's tone did not show the surprise Ray had anticipated. "And who gave you this warning?"

"I hope you won't insist upon my answering that, sir. I'd only get—get someone else into trouble. It's simply that this person informed me of a telephone conversation between Mr. Tracy and Bixler in which Tracy suggested that accidents are not unusual around steel plants, and that I might have an accident. I've already had two narrow escapes."

The General's face was blank and expressionless, but there was a flicker of amusement in the deep black eyes. "I see! Well, I won't insist that you call your informant by name, Locke. Conversations overheard in Tracy's office lead to only one conclusion. If he wishes true privacy, Tracy should have the door between his office and Harris' walled up. Miss North doesn't seem to miss very much going on."

"I didn't say it was Miss North," Ray objected.

U. G. Flint eyed him shrewdly. "A young man's heart frequently overrules his head when a pretty girl is involved."

"What do you mean, sir?" Ray was conscious that color was rising in his pale cheeks, a dead give-away in spite of his resolution not to betray the girl's confidence.

"Use your head," the General said severely. "Why do you suppose the girl was at the laboratory that night?"

"I don't know. Do you?"

"The reason is fairly obvious. But never mind about that now. Go on with your story."

Ray told how he had not put much stock in the warning, but after his encounter with Bixler had decided to keep an eye on Tracy. He related his discovery of the checker-work laboratory and the brass box in the furnace flue.

The General sat in silence for several moments. "Let me get this straight," he said finally. "I'm not a steel man, as I told you, Locke. I'm not sure I quite understand this business of the underground room."

"It isn't exactly underground," Ray explained. "It's really on the ground floor of the Open Hearth plant. Modern plants are built on what is called the two-level type. The furnaces themselves are on the second floor. Behind them and underneath, are these so-called checker-works. The idea is to lead the hot gases of combustion through the brickwork and heat the masonry to a very high temperature. Then the incoming gas and air are routed through the hot checkers and thus preheated. It prevents a great deal of heat from being wasted."

U. G. Flint nodded. "I understand now. It's simply the regenerative principle used in many other kinds of industrial furnaces."

"That's right, sir."

"What," the General asked, "do you make of the laboratory equipment in that place?"

Ray said, "It looks as if the old chambers have been fitted up for some sort of research—probably a study of the gases of combustion. That would explain the connection with the active checker-work adjoining."

The General nodded. "Exactly. And I'm inclined to think we meet up again with Keene's 'key to the locke'...spelled with an *e*. In other words—Nitrogen. Those plant layouts of Rjukan and Notodden open up broad vistas."

"What could they have to do with it?"

"Maybe everything. Rjukan and Notodden were both plants which operated twenty years or more on the Birkeland-Eyde method for fixation of atmospheric nitrogen. That's an electric arc method long since outmoded. Ten or fifteen years ago both plants were converted to the more economical Haber process."

Ray said, "I still don't see the connection."

"You ought to know more about them than I do," the General said accusingly. "You've had a first class technical education. My schooling wasn't handed to me on a silver platter. I had to get out and root for mine—the hard way. I know very little about steel, but I did quite a bit of work for my people during the war in connection with the nitrogen industry."

Ray's curiosity got the better of him. "If you're not a steel man, sir, what..."

A slow grin spread over the General's broad features. "Technically I'm supposed to be a banker. Actually, I'm the fellow who always has the dirty work dropped into his lap."

Ray didn't get it, but be let it go at that. He didn't want the General to think he was trying to pry into things which were none of his concern.

Flint went on, speaking slowly and patiently. "You must remember that until comparatively recent years, the chief source of manufactured nitrogen was ammonium sulphate from the by-product coke ovens, meaning principally from the steel industry. Of course, I'm speaking of artificially produced nitrogen and not of the vast natural deposits of sodium nitrate shipped to this country from Chile."

Ray said, "I knew about that at one time, but I'll have to admit I'm a bit hazy on the whole subject of nitrogen now."

"Since the first World War," the General went on, "the world supply of nitrogen comes almost entirely from fixation of atmospheric nitrogen. The first process developed was this Birkeland-Eyde method. Then came the cyanamide process and lastly the Haber process. I'm sure you can now see the significance of the drawings you found in this checker-work affair."

"No, sir," Ray admitted. "I still don't get it at all."

"Then, young man, you must have little conception of the vital importance of the nitrogen industry." The General spoke severely. "You probably don't realize it, but the current history of the world has been shaped to a considerable extent by the problem of nitrogen supply. Modern war could not be waged without an abundant supply of nitrogen."

Ray said, "You mean because nitrogen is the foundation of the explosives industry?"

"Right. Nearly all modern high explosives are nitrogen compounds. Few persons know how close the Germans came to winning World War I just on that account."

Obviously he wanted to go ahead and talk about it. Ray said, politely, "How was that, sir?"

"At that time the Allies were dependent upon Chilean nitrate for their nitric acid requirements, which meant they were eight thousand miles from their source of supply. When German squadrons began to menace Chilean coastal waters, the Allies suddenly realized the danger of being dependent upon a remote source for such a vital material. The development of an adequate manufactured supply dates from that time. Our people began to rush work on the atmospheric fixation plant at Muscle Shoals. The Chilean supply was not endangered again during that war, however."

"You believe the Germans lost the war because their own supply of nitrogen was insufficient?"

"No. Germany had a plentiful supply, thanks to Professor Fritz Haber who discovered a method of making by-product ammonia from coal. They didn't dare go to war until they did have. It would have been suicidal. There might have been no nitric acid for munitions and no fertilizer for German fields. In my opinion the war was delayed for that reason, until German nitrate plants had achieved sufficient production to assume the risk. Yes, if it hadn't been for Professor Haber, the history of the last thirty years might be vastly different."

Ray waited, but the General had apparently finished his lecture. Ray moved restlessly on the yellow leather lounge. "An interesting bit of history," he ventured finally. "But where does it tie in with the Ironton Works of American-Consolidated Steel today?"

U. G. Flint got to his feet and began to pace the sitting room with measured strides. "If I knew that," he admitted, "I think I'd know everything necessary to wind up this investigation. Can't you see the fascinating range of possibilities, Locke?"

Ray nodded. "I get your point now. Something in connection with nitrogen is going on around Ironton."

"Something big," the General amended. "A lot bigger than surface indications. We've got to find out what."

"But how can we do that?"

"First by continuing our patient spade work, next, by stirring our lazy brain cells." Flint stopped in front of Ray, feet apart as if bracing himself. "I'm going to have a personal look at that place under the Open Hearth. As I remarked before, I'm greatly intrigued with the possible new avenues of investigation suggested by those drawings of nitrogen plants."

"There's another thing I think you should know about, sir." Ray told of his visit to the public library and his discovery that Ashley had not been there the night before. "What do you think about that, Mr. Flint?"

"No thinking is necessary," the General declared. "Obviously the man lied."

"That means…"

"It means Ashley lied—nothing else. It proves Ashley was not downtown when he said he was, but that time was four or five hours prior to Walter Keene's death. Ashley could have been home in bed, as he said he was, at two o'clock in the morning."

Ray asked, "What do you wish me to do now, Mr. Flint?"

"Keep on as you have. You've been a real help."

Ray grimaced. "Okay. Unless I happen to get knocked off by my pal Bixler."

"You'll have to look after yourself. Keep your eyes open."

"That," Ray promised, "is something I very definitely intend to do. Bixler won't get another crack at me."

On the way down to the street in the red plush elevator, Ray consulted his dice again. He was sorry he did, for again they turned up the persistent one and two spots.

TEN

Ray was pulling tensile tests for Gaylord with the big Norton machine when Leonard Tracy walked into the testing lab next morning. The General Superintendent wore a new, light tan suit of tropical worsted. In his lapel was a pink rosebud. Standing so the ugly burn on his throat and right jaw was not visible to Ray, Tracy looked very much the Beau Brummel.

"How's the new job going?" he asked cordially. "How're you making out, Ray?"

Ray grinned. "Only one employee has a better job!"

Tracy frowned faintly. "One employee?"

Still grinning, Ray pointed to Oscar, the laboratory cat, who lay stretched full length on the table beside the test pieces. "The mouse business is booming," he said.

The cat did, in fact, look fat and sleek. Tracy's face cleared. He ran his hand gently over the little animal's soot-grimed white fur. "I'm really delighted that we could move you over here," he told Ray warmly. "It's so much more suitable for your training and background. It actually hurt me to put my old friend's son into an unskilled laborer's job."

"Don't feel that way, Mr. Tracy," Ray protested. "I was glad to get any work at all in Ironton."

Which of them was being hypocritical? Ray wondered. Was Tracy's friendliness a mask for deadly intent, as Jackie North's warning and the encounter with Bixler in the rail mill seemed to indicate? Or had Ray made an ungrateful sneak of himself by skulking at the heels of a man who had befriended him, spying upon his actions and expressing his suspicions to Ulysses G. Flint?

"I had to start you where I did," Tracy went on, as if trying to justify himself. "I'm just a young fellow trying to get along. I might bust myself higher than a kite if I made a bad impression on the big boys in New York."

That line of sales talk sounded corny, coming as it did from a sixty-thousand-a-year executive.

"But when the General says okay"—Tracy waved his hand airily—"then okay it is!"

Ray seized the opportunity Tracy had given him. "Please tell me just who the General is. I thought at first he was an American-Consolidated official, but he says he isn't a steel man."

A smile crinkled the comers of Leonard Tracy's mouth, the cleft of his chin deepened. "Ulysses G. Flint," he told Ray, "is a personage. He's a natural phenomenon and a law unto himself."

Ray continued to regard Tracy questioningly.

"The General," Tracy explained, "is confidential investigator for P. J. Gorman and Company. Some call him head of the Wall Street Gestapo!"

"Is he a retired army man?"

Tracy's smile broadened. "The title is purely honorary. Everyone calls him General because of the Ulysses G."

"But what," Ray asked, "is his connection with American-Consolidated?"

"You know your economic history!" Tracy said. "American-Consolidated is one of the great combines originally formed by Gorman and Company. They still hold enormous blocks of our common stock and are probably the greatest single power on our Board, as they are on the Boards of so many of the country's largest corporations."

"Mr. Flint must be a very important man, then," Ray said thoughtfully.

"Important! Let me tell you, Ray, there are mighty few men in America who would care to test their strength against the General…and the General's connections."

"No wonder, then," Ray said, thinking aloud, "the local police were willing to give him a free hand in the investigation of Walter Keene's death."

Leonard Tracy's smile vanished. "It seems strange to me," he said, "that the General would tie himself down with a routine police case like the murder of a plant chemist."

Ray thought of what the General had told him about "his people's" concern over falsified tests at Ironton.

"Perhaps Mr. Flint didn't come here just on Keene's account," he said.

"I *know* he didn't. He arrived the afternoon before we knew about Keene. I had a note from New York instructing me to provide the General with a private office and to hold myself in readiness to do anything he requested. There was no further explanation." A worried frown spread across Tracy's distinguished features. He dropped his voice to a confidential level. "I don't know why Ulysses Flint came to Ironton, but I can guess. This is strictly off the record, Ray!"

"Of course."

"I have an idea the General's visit may have something to do with Quentin Harris. I don't care much for Harris and New York knows it."

"Is that so?" Ray endeavored to convey just the right shade of respectful interest."

"Harris didn't click with me from the very first," Tracy confided. "He's inclined to be insubordinate. Take the way he acted when I told him to arrange for you on Quirk's payroll. I can sense his hidden unfriendliness. It's nothing definite, you understand, but I frequently get that impression from his general attitude."

"If you feel that way about your own assistant, why don't you get rid of him?" Ray asked boldly.

Tracy's gray-green eyes were shrewd and suddenly wary. "It isn't quite that easy. You see, Harris was sent here, put in a very important position by New York. They told me they had a lot of confidence in his ability.

"As a matter of fact, Quentin Harris is a plugger and he gets the job done. It wouldn't be good organization politics to complain about him to the boys in New York. They're very quick to pick up impressions. I wouldn't want them to get any wrong ideas about my own cooperation. Sometime I'm going to have a chance to get my ideas about him across in a subtle way. A thing like that has to be handled delicately."

Ray said, "I can see your point."

"Organization politics is important," Tracy said. "Some men never seem to realize just how important, and then they wonder why they've missed the boat. Organization politics has a large part to play in the career of almost every man…above a certain level." The General Superintendent straightened his shoulders. "Well, I've got to get along, Ray. Want to have a talk with Clara Dunne this morning about the Keene affair. I've just begun to get a vague idea that maybe Harris had a hand in the mess." Sudden sparks flashed deep in Tracy's eyes. "Maybe," he added slyly, "this whole mess may prove Harris' finish."

He turned toward the stairs. The red scar with its puckered white edges was now visible. In spite of himself, Ray felt a sudden revulsion.

After Tracy had gone, Ray turned back to his work. For more than an hour he broke test specimens in the Norton machine. He was finishing the last batch when Tracy came back downstairs.

This time the General Superintendent did not come through the physical lab but went out the side door near Ashley's office. Ray noticed, as the man strode briefly across his line of vision, that Tracy's mouth was set in a grim line and there was an angry light in his eyes.

* * * *

During lunch hour, Ray went to the plate mill, searching out a quiet corner for his half hour nap.

Again he chose the end where the finished plates were piled. At the other end of the long mill building, the recuperative furnaces were winking as glowing slabs moved from them to the roughing rolls. The middle of the structure was a bedlam of roaring machinery, all busily engaged in squeezing thick slabs into thin plate steel.

Fiery sheets of the heavy metal whisked back and forth in seemingly interminable passes through the massive rolls. Whistle signals shrilled. Shears, like gigantic guillotine blades, slashed through hot plates as a knife would slice a loaf of bread.

An overhead crane was shuttling about as usual, at the end of the building where Ray stood, engaged in its endless task of piling and re-piling the cold finished plates.

He stood for a moment watching it. The wire rope cables drooped to the dirt floor of the mill as workmen secured chains around the edges of the plates to be moved, then drew taut again as each tremendous burden was raised and carried across the width of the mill.

Ray thought of the times when he had inspected plates for the railroad, how he had looked at the top surface, for "snakes" and "pits" and other defects. Then the plate had been raised by the crane, banging suspended on claw-like books from the overhead crane, for him to inspect the under surface.

He'd had an understanding about that with his boss in the railroad's Department of Tests.

"I'll go over the tops of all plates thoroughly," he'd said, "but I won't go under them. If that isn't satisfactory, I'm not the man you want on this job."

It wasn't strictly according to the rules, but it had been satisfactory. Only one plate needed to slip and fall. Old mill hands can tell what happens when a plate does fall on a man.

Ray selected a small pile of plates near the side of the building. He was just getting ready to curl up when he saw the crane come over again.

"You fellows going to move this stack?" he called to the straw boss in charge of the work gang.

The man grinned. "You're okay, pal. We ain't gonna touch that there iron a while."

Ray settled himself on the smooth, cold surface. He went to sleep quickly, a deep, dreamless slumber this time, undisturbed by the crash and clatter around him.

His reduced rest schedule eliminated all danger of insomnia. But habit kept an alarm clock wound and set in Ray's subconscious, to wake him at exactly the right moment.

This time the alarm never went off. Five minutes before it was due, Ray awoke, scrambling from his hard couch in mortal terror.

From the sling of the traveling crane, not more than a dozen feet from him, the plates were showering to the ground in a thunderous uproar of cascading steel. They struck other plates in the piles beneath. Some of them turned end over end in the act of falling. Sparks flashed.

One of the falling plates struck the pile on which Ray was lying, not more than inches from his head. The edge, sharp as a giant razor, cut a silvery gash in the surface beside him.

Ray leaped to his feet, shrinking back as close to the wall as he could get. His mind recalled, even before the last plate hit the dirt, the grease spot from the chicken bone which he had seen a few days before. If one of those toppling plates struck him, the mill hands would have a nasty job tidying this end of the mill.

Then the gang of men was clustering around excitedly while the crane operator leaned from his bridge, looking down. Ray stood stock still for a moment. When he stopped shaking, he went over to join the workmen.

He'd had plenty of experience judging metal by the appearance of its fracture. He looked now at the edges of the broken wire rope cable.

The inner strands had a clean metallic break, but the outer strands showed a peculiar smooth appearance. Ray knew what that appearance signified.

They had been eaten through by acid.

* * * *

When quitting time rolled around, Ray did not leave the laboratory building. More than ever he wanted to search the place. But since his previous two attempts, late at night, had netted about the same degree of privacy he might have expected in the concourse of New York's Grand Central Station, he thought he would try a different time, when any Test Department people who planned to work at night would be out to dinner.

Most of the lab employees were quick to depart on the very stroke of the clock. The inevitable few stragglers remained, but gradually even these left. Ray waited patiently, lining up his work for the morning, until finally he thought he was alone in the building.

He'd start with the chemical lab and work down, he decided, and turned to the stairs. Halfway up he discovered that someone was still around. Indistinct voices came from Clara Dunne's office near the head of the steps, low voices which stopped abruptly as Ray appeared.

Leonard Tracy was closed into the tiny, boxlike space with Clara Dunne. Through the glass panels Ray could see that the General

Superintendent's customary suavity had disappeared. Lines ridged the man's forehead and anger twisted his mouth.

Clara, also, appeared upset about something. There was less color than usual in her plump cheeks. They looked thinner on account of the rigid set of her jaw. It was the first time Ray had ever seen her wear other than her habitual calm expression. It occurred to him that her display of emotion was not at all unbecoming.

The sudden silence, and the way both of them watched him as he neared the top of the stairs, gave Ray an acute feeling that he was an unwelcome intruder on a very private conversation.

"I wanted to see the chemical results on that last batch of driving wheels," he said in a spur-of-the-moment explanation as Clara opened the door and gave him a questioning glance.

"They're not ready yet," she told him a trifle curtly.

He said, "Okay, I'll get them tomorrow," then turned and went back downstairs hastily.

With sudden impatience, Ray decided he would not wait for them to leave. Someone else was likely to come back by that time and he might again miss his opportunity.

He went into Ashley's office. Dying daylight still persisted, but the vast shadows of the mill buildings were beginning to disintegrate into shapelessness as the dusk closed in. Ray pulled down Ashley's shades, turned on the lights. He left the door into the hall open so he would know if Clara or Tracy came downstairs.

He pulled out the top drawer of Ashley's private file, began to thumb rapidly through the folders inside. He found nothing of interest to himself.

He had started on the third drawer when the squeaky hinge of the door at the side corridor entrance warned him. He heard it squeak open, then shut again, stealthily. Very soft footsteps whispered along the bare boards of the connecting hallway.

Ray slid the file drawer shut noiselessly. He jumped for the light switch, plunged the room into darkness. He had just time enough to slip through the door and into the adjoining clerical office before the furtive footsteps reached the turn of the hall.

Flattened against the wall just inside the clerical office, Ray heard Ashley's door close quietly. The faint *snick* of the light switch reached his ears through the thin panel and then the sound of file drawers being pulled rapidly open and shut.

Ray was thinking fast. If it were Ashley himself who had returned, the drawn shades in the private office would be a dead give-away. And if Ashley's suspicions of Ray reached a positive stage, it could prove very embarrassing, not only to Ray, but to the General as well.

Ray wondered if he might be able to get past the closed door of the private office without being caught in the attempt. He decided to take the chance. But in the very act of slipping out once more into the hallway, he heard the faint *tap-tap* of high heels approaching through the physical laboratory.

He shrank back again into the clerical office, as the heels clicked into the corridor. A light tap sounded on Ashley's door. A guarded, feminine voice said, "Chris, are you there?"

Ray couldn't distinguish the voice, but that it was Ashley who replied there could be no doubt.

"We won't be safe in here tonight," the man said in a husky whisper. "Someone's been snooping. Must have left just as I came in. We'd better get out of here."

The footsteps, no longer guarded, moved in Ray's direction. The hall light came on. Ray looked around frantically. In the crowded room there was absolutely no place for him to hide. In desperation, he dropped to hands and knees, crawled behind one of the three stenographic desks just as Ashley came to the door.

The ceiling light in the office flashed on. Ray crouched, motionless, holding his breath. One step into the office and Ashley could not fail to see him.

Ashley did not take that step. The lights snapped off again; the Engineer of Tests moved back along the hall.

Still on hands and knees, Ray crawled hastily to the door. The girl was in the very act of rounding the corner turn. All Ray saw was a head covered in a gay bandanna and a brief splotch of red skirt. But Ashley's silhouette against the wall was unmistakable. It's wisp of beard, magnified by the downward slant of the electric light, made Ashley's shadow look like a grotesque caricature of Uncle Sam.

At that moment Leonard Tracy came downstairs. Ashley's silhouette, still visible to Ray, although the man himself was around the bend of the hall, remained stationary against the wall as the General Superintendent strode away purposefully through the physical lab.

Although consumed with curiosity about Ashley and his companion, Ray realized that a check on Tracy's moves was a matter of more concern to him than satisfying his inquisitiveness.

But he could not leave the clerical office without almost certainly being seen by Ashley. The man's motionless shadow showed that, whatever he was doing tonight with the help of the girl, the Engineer of Tests did not care to advertise his presence any more than did Ray. And by lingering as he did in the side corridor, Ashley unknowingly held Ray securely trapped.

The moment Tracy disappeared, the couple moved tentatively from their hiding place, but ducked back hastily as purposeful footsteps sounded overhead and Clara Dunne came down from upstairs. She went straight out, but it was at least five more minutes before Ashley and his feminine companion went on along the corridor and the tell-tale squeak of the door hinge informed Ray he could safely emerge from hiding.

He rushed out then through the physical lab. He still wanted to find Tracy, but with the head start the General Superintendent had gained, Ray feared it would be impossible.

Coming out by the side of the forge shop, Ray looked around quickly. By this time it had grown quite dark. No one was in sight.

Tracy could have gone in almost any direction. If he had intended to leave the plant, his most probable route would be between the blooming mill and the billet mill. Ray started in that direction on the run.

He cut around the end of the billet mill and turned to the side of the slabbing mill. Even if Tracy were not far ahead of him, it would be easy to lose a man among the many buildings crowded into this part of the Works.

Two men were standing halfway along the end of the slabbing mill as Ray reached that open stretch. He stepped back quickly. When he looked around the corner a moment later, the men had separated.

Light from the slabbing mill reflected on eyeglasses and Ray recognized Benjamin Gaylord's bony skull-like features as the Chief Inspector hurried past the end of the structure and disappeared. The other man came plowing around the corner near Ray.

It was the heavy, monk-like Quentin Harris, coatless as usual and chewing on his inevitable cigar stump. He did not see Ray and barged ahead toward the plate mill. There was no sign anywhere of Leonard Tracy.

Ray broke into a run. He couldn't have lost him by a great distance. But the General Superintendent might have turned into any of the various mills, or he could have doubled back in the direction from which he had come, on the other side of the rolling mill buildings.

Beyond the slabbing mill various types of merchant mills were housed. The nearest was the bar mill. Ray took the corner fast, straight into a slight, flying figure which hit him squarely, almost knocking him from his feet and driving the breath completely from his lungs.

It was entirely dark now, but an early moon was already luminous overhead. Moonglow, together with the electric light which spilled from the noisy, clanging bar mill, gave Ray a good look at the person with whom he had collided. It was Jackie North.

The girl scrambled hastily to her feet without a word. She was panting, more from fright, it seemed, than from exertion. The harsh glare from the bar mill revealed the pallor of her face, the rouge standing out in dark splotches against the whiteness of her cheeks.

"Miss North!" Ray began gaspingly. "What..."

He broke off, shouted, "Jackie! Wait!" as she began to run.

By the time he had recovered from his surprise and started after her, he found she had already vanished somewhere among the mill buildings.

Ray shrugged and started again along the side of the bar mill. He was afraid now that he had definitely lost Tracy. That would mean another long wait outside the executive offices again to pick up the General Superintendent, or, more likely, a completely wasted evening so far as learning anything new was concerned.

He reached the end of the bar mill. In a shed-like addition beyond the door of the structure, bars of various sizes and lengths were kept in wooden racks. In front of the racks were alligator shears used for cutting the bars to desired lengths. The shear blades, electrically operated, moved up and down in rhythmical strokes like the monotonous opening and shutting of a four-foot pair of scissors.

Just beside the shear, half squatting, half stooping, was the figure of a man—a large powerfully built man, far different from the slender Leonard Tracy. The man twisted about, startled, at the sound of Ray's feet on the cinders which carpeted the ground.

Ray also stopped dead, frozen with astonishment.

The moon shone down palely, providing just enough illumination for him to recognize the convulsive twist of the facial tic which drew Glenn Cannon's profile into a simulated leer.

An exclamation burst from Ray's lips. "Cannon!"

Cannon straightened swiftly, leaped away like a frightened animal. Overcoming his initial surprise, Ray started after him, then caught a glimpse in the moon' light of the thing on the ground over which Cannon had been stooping. He stopped short.

He had caught up with Leonard Tracy.

The man's handsome face was turned to Ray as if watching, while Ray stooped in the same spot where Cannon had been. By a trick of reflection, the moonbeams made Tracy's eyes gleam like those of a cat caught in the headlights of an automobile.

But the eyes were not watching Ray. Nor did they gleam with inner fire. They were dead eyes. And the head stood by itself, without a body, just below the restlessly moving jaws of the alligator shears.

Tracy's body lay on the other side of the shear blades. Moonrays glistened reddish-black on the wet cinders into which the life blood of the General Superintendent had drained. With an oddly pathetic gesture they touched the rosebud in the lapel of the dead man's once handsome tan suit.

Ray bent over the headless corpse in frozen horror. Invisible fingers squeezed his stomach; he felt swift nausea rising in his throat.

And as he crouched, still under the paralysis of disgust and terror, a burly figure stepped from the darkness of the shed-like storage space where the bars were racked. Moonlight shone on the nickel-plating of a police revolver.

"Get your hands up," the bull voice of "Windpipe" Bixler ordered. "This time I caught you red-handed, Locke!"

ELEVEN

The sudden appearance of the company cop was like a shot of adrenalin to Ray. His paralyzed muscles functioned once more. Slowly he straightened, raised his hands over his head.

"You ain't gonna have no more chances to go around murderin' people in this here plant," Bixler promised. His voice held a low, growling threat.

"I just found Tr—found this, myself," Ray started to protest. "You must have seen me come here, not more than a minute ago."

Bixler said, "Don't try to talk yourself out of it, bud! Not with me." There was something implacable in his tone, and a note which sounded almost like triumph.

"I don't intend to waste time with you," Ray retorted. "I want to see Mr. Flint."

"Tryin' to make more trouble, eh?" Bixler spoke slowly, as if he were thinking out loud. "Maybe the easiest way to settle this would be for you to get shot while resistin' arrest. Yeah…"

The murder in Bixler's thoughts was as clear to Ray as type on a printed page. Only the slow functioning of the company cop's mind delayed his homicidal action.

Shot while resisting arrest. That, Ray knew, would be his epitaph. He would never reach Ironton's gates, nor communicate with U. G. Flint. In another second Bixler would shoot.

Ray threw himself violently to one side even as the thought swirled through his mind. He ducked while Bixler's words were still forming, his finger tightening on the trigger of the gun. Then Bixler fired, the bullet whispering away harmlessly into the night.

Panic and instinct for self-preservation gave Ray a speed of which he had never before been capable. He fled blindly, without definite destination ahead. To elude Bixler…that was his only thought. He had a vague hope that he might lose the man somewhere inside the maze of mill buildings.

A kaleidoscope of half-perceived scenes revolved around him. He fled through the Bessemer plant, past forty-foot tongues of flame, with the earth shaking under the ear-splitting roar of air blasting through the mouth of the converter under terrific pressure and hot sparks, like fire-flies, dancing through the vast building from roof trusses to the dirt floor.

He dodged across the hot plates of the soaking pits, where glowing ingots like chunks of white metallic ice were dangling from overhead cranes. All the time Bixler hung grimly behind him.

Darting in through a side entrance to the sheet mill, Ray found him-self unexpectedly trapped. Directly in front of him was a train of rollers carrying its continuous strip of thin sheet from the finishing roll pass to the flying shears.

The flying shears themselves, heavy knife blades working continu-ally up and down under the drive of a steam cylinder, were at Ray's right. And the space between shears and mill end was blocked by the thick pile of cut sheets which tumbled automatically from the roll table at the delivery end of the shears.

The way to get across to the other mill entrance was over a catwalk a hundred feet back in the other direction. Ray had turned the wrong way upon entering the mill. Now he was pocketed, unable to retrace his steps because Bixler was already barging through the aisle behind him, between the mill wall and the roll table.

Bixler was slowing, raising the gun. Ray had lost count of the shots remaining in the cop's revolver, but the situation was hopeless. Bixler would be shooting from point blank range and there was ample time for him to reload.

There was one possibility: If he could leap the six feet over the roll table to the other side, he would escape the trap, while Bixler would be forced to retreat via the catwalk to get across the barrier.

But to leap the roll table meant a truly desperate chance. If he missed, even by inches, he would either be fried alive on the hot sheets or sliced in half under the flying shears—perhaps both.

There was no time for pondering a decision. Anyhow, he had no real choice. It was either risk a terrible death in an all-out bid for freedom, or stand his ground and be cut down by the fire of the murderous company cop.

Ray gave a tremendous leap, putting all his remaining strength into a headlong dive over the roll table and across the moving steel sheet. The sheet was cooling, but it still glowed a dull angry red. Ray could feel scorching heat strike upward at his body as he plunged over. The downward slash of the shear blades, as brilliant electric light struck the moving knives from above, was like the sudden flash of a mirror. So close were they that Ray's plunging body almost brushed them as he catapulted across. Sparks struck from the guide frame of the shears as one of Bixler's steel-jacketed bullets glanced from the metal.

Then he had fallen, all in one piece, in the dirt on the other side of that flat, red-glowing steel sheet. And Bixler was shouting in a bull voice of rage and frustration from the other side of the roll table.

Ray picked himself up hastily, gasping, almost sick from shock and exertion. For an instant he thought Bixler was going to risk the leap after him. The burly, blue-uniformed figure did hesitate momentarily. Then Bixler thought better of the reckless impulse and raced back toward the catwalk. Workmen on the other side of the sheet mill were looking up from their labor, mouths gaping at the scene just enacted before their eyes.

His narrow escape filled Ray with a sudden dread of the confined mill structures. He headed for the open, toward the cinder dumps and billet piles. His suicidal leap across the flying shears had given him a greatly increased lead over his pursuer. He hoped fervently that the faint moonlight would be insufficient to reveal him again to Bixler.

The splice bar mill was dark. Evidently its run of bars had been completed and work shut down temporarily before starting some other railroad's order. Ray remembered how he used to get rail joints, splice bars as they were called in the mills, by the carload lot when he had worked for Transcontinental.

In those days he had gangs of men loading the cars for him, while he sometimes caught one of his brief naps in the rookery of dingy offices on the upper floor of the mill building. Those offices, when the mill was not in operation pending a change-over of rolls, were a deserted place.

It occurred to Ray, in a flash of inspiration, that this might be an ideal place for him to hide, if Bixler did not see him go there.

He thought he was successful. In darkness like the inside of a bat roost, Ray located the cupped wooden stairs leading from the bottom portion of the splice bar mill to the upstairs offices. He risked a match for an instant at the head of the steps.

The tiny flare showed him a small barren room, just to the right of the stair landing. There was nothing in it except an old battered desk, thick with dust, and an old leather couch like the one in Christopher Ashley's office.

Evidently, this place had not been used for a long time. Scraps of steel were scattered on the floor; defective splice bars, rejects from some past inspection, lay along the walls. Some of these rejects, it occurred to Ray sadly, might even be relics of his own happier days as a Transcontinental inspector.

He shook out the match, stretched full length on the couch. His lungs were still laboring painfully from his long sprint, and his stomach felt cloudy, unsettled. He marveled that neither his discovery of Tracy's headless corpse nor his own plunge across the flying shears had made him actually sick.

Just when his breathing was under control once more and he was congratulating himself upon having eluded Bixler, a dim light filtered into the room from below the stairs. It wavered for a moment, then heavy footsteps sounded on the wooden treads. The flashlight beam grew stronger.

Hastily, Ray slipped from the couch to the floor, squeezing beneath the sagging springs. He was just in time. Peering from his place of concealment, he saw a big form loom from the stair landing. Ray's prone position gave him a worm's-eye view of Bixler, gigantic, formidable, yet at the same time insubstantial in the diffused glow of the flashlight.

He shrank back as close to the wall as he could, not daring to breathe. Bixler's heavy tread made the ancient flooring tremble. The flashlight beam almost touched Ray with its probing finger as it swung around briefly.

Then Bixler went into the room adjoining. Ray could hear the big cop moving around all the empty offices in the old rookery. His nerves were relaxing again when a new thought threw him into a fresh agony of apprehension.

His footprints in the heavy dust were bound to show, straight from the door to in front of the couch where he had wiped up the place with his clothes while crawling beneath it.

It was miraculous Bixler had not found him at once. The reason, Ray knew, was simply that the man had not yet taken time for a careful search. He was making a hurried first survey. And when he failed to find his victim, he would retrace his steps, looking more carefully in each empty office.

The fact that Bixler had come to the splice bar mill showed that either the treacherous moonlight or the match he had lighted had betrayed Ray. If the burly cop found him beneath the couch, it required little imagination to know what would happen.

Sweat burst out in big globules on Ray's forehead. He faced a veritable Hobson's choice. If he remained where he was, Bixler would almost certainly return to blast him into ribbons. If he tried to leave the place, the company cop could scarcely fail to hear him moving over the creaky floors.

Action, Ray decided, was preferable to cowering rabbit-like, awaiting the slow approach of the inevitable. At least if he were on his feet, he would have the chance to grapple with Bixler in a final effort to save his life, although the outcome of such a struggle was subject to little doubt. Bixler was a powerful bruiser. Ray, slim and small-boned, would be like Tom Thumb in the grasp of the ogre.

Swiftly he wriggled from his hiding place and crossed the room on all fours. Bixler, with his light, was in the room farthest from the stairs. Ray came to his feet, crept to the landing. He tested each step like a swimmer in icy water. Then, gaining confidence as he went down, he moved more swiftly. Two-thirds of the way down a board screeched agonized protest.

Bixler was at the stair head almost instantly. His flashlight beam speared Ray like a butterfly on a pin. The crack of his revolver echoed through the empty offices like the detonation of high explosive.

Ray took the remaining steps in one wild leap, as Bixler hammered down behind him. Then there were cinders under his feet again. He turned back toward the mill buildings, stumbled on uneven ground and fell sprawling.

By the time he regained his feet, Bixler had cut between him and his line of retreat. Ray swerved toward the coal docks, avoiding the blast furnaces.

There were many men around the furnaces. If Bixler saw him go there, it would be possible to phone ahead from a plant connection in the splice bar mill. Then, Ray knew, he might find himself bottled up, with the odds against him overwhelming.

But before he realized it, Ray was pocketed, his line of flight blocked except for the coal docks and the inlet. Aside from the short stretch along the docks themselves, the Ironton Works, even along the curve of the waterway by the Bessemer and Open Hearth, was surrounded completely by high fences topped with barbed wire.

Ray remembered the gurgling suck of black, oily water against the slimy wharf piling under the drag of the heavy current. The tidal inlet formed a raceway too swift even for the most powerful swimmer to risk the quarter mile crossing.

Better to turn and grapple with Bixler, he decided, than to suffocate in the scum and filth of what was no better than an open sewer. Still running, Ray bent to snatch a big lump of cinder from the ground. It would be better than no weapon at all if he weren't successful in eluding Bixler.

A small concrete building like a pump house stood just back from the docks, housing a battery of transformers for the power lines overhead. Clusters of heavy cables hung in a graceful catenary curve from the lattice-work of transmission towers above.

Ray ducked into the concrete room and looked around frantically, seeking a place to hide. The walls seemed stern and pitiless in their implacable smoothness. But there were dark shadows behind the row of transformers which might offer temporary protection. He slipped into them just as Bixler turned the corner of the transformer station. Instinctively, Ray shrank closer to the wall, trying to make himself one with it. Shock mingled with relief as he felt it give way against his back. A narrow black opening yawned in the deepest shadow. He stepped into it as "Windpipe" Bixler came through the door.

TWELVE

Behind Ray, the opening through which he had come was a faint yellow-gray outline as Bixler's flashlight circled the transformer room. Ahead was total blackness.

He felt his way forward, putting half a dozen steps between himself and the menace of Bixler's gun. His hands touched lead-covered cables…a number of them, hunched together.

There were pipes also, together with the power cables, along a concrete shelf which dipped on a steep angle into the earth. Beside the shelf, the space was narrow. There was just room enough for a man to squeeze through, not quite enough for him to stand erect.

At last Ray knew how Glenn Cannon had managed to enter and leave the Ironton Works without being seen. Undoubtedly, he reasoned, this small tunnel carried power lines to the old blast furnaces across the inlet, probably connected with the substation over there.

The blast furnaces, long outmoded, had been stripped of everything worth salvage and abandoned years ago. Now they were slowly rusting into oblivion. But the conduits, with the narrow tunnel providing access for a linesman in case of trouble, still supplied some of Ironton's power requirements—a fact largely forgotten by all save the plant's electricians, and by Cannon.

The light from Bixler's flash had vanished. Probably the company cop was roaming the area near the coal docks, wondering how his quarry had managed to vanish. Set back behind the rows of transformers as it was, the slit-like tunnel entrance easily escaped attention unless one happened to face it squarely.

Ray's sense of liberation was almost intoxicating. All he had to do now was follow the tunnel beneath the waters of the inlet and he would be safe at the abandoned blast furnaces, free of the Ironton Works.

He made his way forward, stooping, hand against the concrete wall for guidance. It was some three-eighths of a mile across the inlet at this point. The tunnel's downward dip leveled off after the first two hundred feet.

The tomblike blackness held a damp, musty smell of cobwebs and decay. The air was fetid from lack of adequate ventilation. When he had ventured what he judged was a third of the way across, Ray decided to risk a match.

The feeble flame showed him only a twelve-foot stretch, walled off at each end with sable gloom. There was nothing but cold, blank concrete and the lead-covered conduits on their ledge. The space above the pipes was thick with cobwebs, soot-laden even here, underground. The footway, however, had been brushed clear, evidently by the passage of Glenn Cannon's body.

The match flickered out. Ray moved along. Twenty minutes later he emerged from blackness like a mole from an underground burrow.

His deductions had been correct. The tunnel opened into a one-room concrete building like the one near the coal docks on the other side of the inlet. And overhead transmission towers carried the wires away toward the substation.

Silhouetted against the water by the dying moon, the abandoned furnaces with their batteries of stoves loomed blackly like the high, crenellated wall of a medieval fortress. To Ray, after his swift alternations between hope and despair, their grotesque unreality was no greater than the complete unreality of the entire universe.

The experiences through which he had passed so swiftly were all incredible. A succession of pictures, unbelievable yet true, passed before his inner vision: the iron cage of the penitentiary; that night on the crowded train on the way to Ironton, with its dreams of clearing his reputation; his interview with Leonard Tracy; the General Superintendents unanticipated cordiality; the Open Hearth; Walter Keene's dead body with the shattered skull which seemed intact; General Ulysses G. Flint and his shrewd, penetrating, black eyes; his hairline escape at the rail mill; the checker-work laboratory below Number Twelve furnace; and finally Leonard Tracy's handsome face staring sightlessly from the dirt and cinders.

How long had it been since Tracy had risen from tire swanky, circular desk to greet him with outstretched hand? Only three days ago. Three days! And now Tracy was gone and Ray himself was a hunted fugitive.

The thought cooled Ray's initial feeling of elation over his escape. Now, for the first time, he realized the full menace of the trap into which he had walked with wide open eyes.

Examined coldly, his actions seemed highly questionable. By running from the scene of Leonard Tracy's murder, he had virtually admitted his own guilt. Would anyone, even U. G. Flint, believe that Bixler had really intended to shoot him in the back?

His flight, Ray realized, was almost as incriminating as a written confession. All his efforts to clear himself from complicity in the wreck of *The Prairie Comet* had only involved him more and more deeply in a mesh of crime. If he gave himself up now to the police, he would most certainly be convicted of Tracy's murder. The very least which could happen to him would be the revocation of his parole and another two or three years in the penitentiary.

Suffering a complete reaction to his previous lift of spirits, Ray even found himself wondering if it might not have been better to have gone down inside the gates of Ironton with a slug from Bixler's revolver in his back.

His chin came up. Such thoughts were sheer defeatism. He was guilty of no crime. It was his word against the word of "Windpipe" Bixler, and fortunately, Ulysses G. Flint knew of Bixler's previous attempts against Ray's life. The General was his best, if not his only, chance of clearing himself.

Almost at once, Ray decided he must attempt to see Flint. The General should be told about these latest developments. Furthermore, a police dragnet would be put out for the supposed slayer of Leonard Tracy as soon as Bixler made his lying report. In that case, the most unlikely spot the authorities would look for Ray was in the company of U. G. Flint.

Men were working at the power substation. Ray caught glimpses of them occasionally as they passed under glaring lights near the structural lattice-work of the substation transmission towers. He felt their eyes watching him as he made his way along the line of towering, rusty, blast furnace stoves.

He shook himself angrily. Of course he was completely invisible in the darkness beneath the abandoned furnaces. This was no time to lose his nerve. Nothing but continued courage, even a certain degree of daring, could possibly avert complete disaster.

Some thousand feet behind the old furnaces, a high board fence, surmounted with barbed wire, enclosed the property of American-Consolidated Steel. Time and neglect had rotted the hoards. Ray kicked one loose and squeezed through to the street beyond.

He found himself in a fourth-rate business section. His route to the nearest street car line led past pool-rooms, second-hand shops and cheap eating places. In spite of his continued feeling that everyone was looking at him, nobody actually gave him a second glance. A man in soiled work clothes was no rarity in this portion of the city.

But at the George Washington Hotel, the situation would be reversed. Ray knew he would he inviting attention and possible trouble if he barged into that gilt-and-plush lobby in greasy jeans. Yet he could not risk a return to his rooming house. Bixler had probably already given the alarm, and the police would be sure to look for him first thing at the dreary room.

He solved this problem by buying a fairly presentable business suit in one of the innumerable, late-open, second-hand stores, with money remaining from his pawned wrist watch. The gray color of the suit he selected would help disguise its somewhat frayed coat sleeves and trouser cuffs unless he were subject to minute inspection. That, he felt, was unlikely.

In the back room of the shop, he changed, washed his face and hands, and wrapped his work clothes in a bundle which he left to he picked up later. Then he went on, caught a street car and rode downtown.

He called Flint on a house phone in the hotel lobby. After a short wait the switchboard girl said, "Sorry, 17-D does not answer."

Ray turned to the room desk. The General's key was in the mail box. Ray glanced up at the clock over the marble counter. The hands stood at eight-fifty-three. The fact struck him with a sense of surprise. After what he had been through, midnight would have seemed more reasonable.

Probably the General had lingered at the plant, or maybe he was having a leisurely dinner. The best thing would be to wait.

He crossed to the newsstand, bought an evening paper and settled himself in a chair where he could see the desk and the elevators. The General would have to stop at the desk for his key. Ray spread the paper, screening himself behind it as he waited and watched.

In about twenty minutes, Ray's heart gave a leap and then began to pound heavily. A tall man had come into the lobby. Those sharp, wedge-shaped features belonged unmistakably to Lieutenant Lambert of Homicide. Ray peered guardedly over the edge of his paper as the police detective approached the desk clerk and spoke with the man.

Ray saw the clerk turn to the mail boxes and then back to Lambert. Evidently he was informing the policeman that U. G. Flint was not in. And Lambert, obviously reaching the same decision Ray had reached, walked over toward where Ray was sitting. For a keenly painful instant Ray feared the detective was about to occupy the adjoining chair.

But Lambert finally seated himself a short distance in front of Ray. Facing the desk, the man's back was toward Ray.

Ray got up quickly, turned through a red-carpeted corridor and went out a side entrance to the street. The alarm then had been given and the entire police organization was on the alert. And that meant he was in constantly increasing danger whatever he did.

There was only one sensible conclusion. He would have to hide until such time as he could safely get in touch with U. G. Flint. But where? He thought suddenly of the abandoned blast furnaces where the tunnel under the inlet emerged. Inside one of those furnaces he would have a hiding place where no one would ever think to look.

Ray caught a street car back in that direction. He'd spend the night in the deserted plant, he decided, and try again in the morning to reach the General. In the meantime, he'd get something to eat. He had passed up his dinner for his interrupted effort at searching the test laboratory. Now his stomach was reminding him most uncomfortably of the omission.

Half a block before he reached the rotting board fence, a gaudy green-and-red neon sign bore the single word, *Eat*. Part of the letter *a* was missing. Narrow windows, so covered with grime that the dimly lit interior of the joint was scarcely visible from the street, were set in crumbling frames from which all vestiges of paint had vanished.

Ray shrugged and turned into the place. He did not expect a course dinner; he could get a plate of beans here and that was sufficient. Stale atmosphere, redolent of onions and burned grease, closed about him. At a wooden counter covered with cracked and patched linoleum, two hunkies in overalls were waiting, while the fat Greek proprietor drew coffee from a badly corroded urn.

A row of flimsy booths ranged along the left-hand wall. Ray picked one near the back, brushed away a swarm of flies hovering around the mouth of an almost empty catsup bottle, and waited for the Greek. Low voices came from the booth behind him, a man and a woman in earnest conversation. Ray paid no attention at first until suddenly a name stabbed him into alertness as if a needle had been thrust through the booth partition into his back.

"...too dangerous after this Tracy business tonight!" the masculine voice had declared.

The woman said, "Why don't you just lie low for a few days until I tell you things have quieted down? Then we can try the test lab once more."

Ray got to his feet, stepped to the adjoining booth. As the fragment of overheard conversation had made him suspect, the occupants of the booth were Glenn Cannon and Jackie North.

"You aren't going to try anything once more, either of you," Ray stated flatly. "If you think I'm going to be your fall guy again, you're mistaken."

Both of them looked up at the unexpected interruption. The girl's brown eyes widened, a sudden rush of color flooded her cheeks. Cannon's heavy, dead-pan face twisted instantly into the leer caused by his nervous tic.

The girl began to stammer. "You—you don't understand..."

"I understand all right," Ray said roughly. "I don't know which of you killed Tracy, but that's up to the police to find out." He called loudly to the Greek who was still behind the counter. "Come over here, George!"

Cannon said hastily, "What are you going to do, Locke?"

"Send for the police—right now, before you have a chance to run out on me again."

"Don't go off half-cocked, Ray!" Cannon's tone was urgent; his face twitched violently. "Jackie and I had nothing to do with that—with Tracy. I've been trying to help you as well as myself."

"Nuts!"

"If you'll just sit down and listen to me for a minute…"

"Please!" Jackie implored. "For your own sake."

The Greek, a dirty white apron tied around his pudgy middle, had come over to stand beside Ray. "What you want, mister?"

Ray was thinking quickly. Although convinced in his own mind that he had caught Cannon and the girl cold, it would still be a formidable job to convince the police of his own innocence. Perhaps it would be a smart idea to let these people talk first, before putting himself, along with them, into the hands of the law.

"Bring me a plate of beans and a cup of coffee," he told the Greek and seated himself alongside Cannon, thereby blocking the man into the booth and preventing any thought he may have had of making a break for the door.

"Okay, Cannon," he said as the Greek departed. "Go ahead and talk. But you'd better make it good. I'm not going to lay *my* head on the block for you."

Cannon blinked and twitched, but his voice was low and earnest. "I'm telling you the truth, Ray. Jackie and I just happened to stumble across Tracy's body."

"You surely ducked fast enough!"

"Wouldn't *you* have ducked? With a murder rap pinned on me I'd be sunk. I'd never have a chance to clear myself."

"You've got to believe that we're your friends," Jackie added.

They both sounded sincere. It came to Ray that Cannon's mind actually seemed to work in much the same channels as his own. But he couldn't afford to jump to conclusions.

"Why has Miss North been chasing all around the Ironton Works at night?" he asked sternly.

"Glenn happens to be my favorite cousin," she told him simply. "I know he's innocent and I've been trying to help him prove it. But every time we tried to get into the laboratory"—her tone turned petulant—"you've managed to spoil things for us."

"What were you trying to do at the laboratory? You lied to me," Ray accused. "You told me Harris sent you there."

"He did."

"But you just said…"

"I was framed on that other deal," Cannon interrupted, "the same as you. I thought I might find something in the old records to prove it. If we could get those axle test originals..."

"We wanted to beat Harris to it," Jackie explained. "That's what Harris wanted me to find for him. But I intended to keep watch while Glenn looked through the files."

It didn't seem implausible to Ray, since that was exactly what he had attempted himself. He started to say so, stopped as the Greek appeared again with a plate of wilted looking beans, set the dish in front of Ray with a clatter and wiped his thumb, which had been in the juice, on his spotted apron. A coffee cup, thick as boiler plate, followed the beans to the chipped, porcelain table top.

"You've got a smooth line of talk," Ray admitted when the man had departed. "I'll have to grant that much to both of you."

"You should be able to understand how it feels when everyone doubts you," Jackie said severely. "Actually, if we were unfriendly to you, it would be simple enough to say that we saw you kill Tracy. It would be the testimony of two against one."

"Just as I thought," Ray said bitterly. "You're going to try framing me again." He started to get up.

"I'm just trying to show that we're really friends," Jackie said hastily. "If we can prove Glenn's innocence, we're bound to prove yours at the same time. Can't you see that?"

Cannon said, "Use your head, Ray! If I'd actually been guilty in connection with those defective axles, do you think I'd have left a letter lying around in my desk to nail down the case against me?" He leaned across the table and tapped with the handle of his knife on the table top to emphasize his point. "That letter was a forgery, Ray. It was put there by someone who wanted me out of the way." His face twitched again in an uncontrollable spasm. "I've never been able to understand who could have wanted to do that or why."

Ray sat silent for a moment. The point was a good one, one which he had pondered himself without finding a satisfactory explanation. The more Cannon talked, the more convincing an impression he made upon Ray.

As Ray hesitated, Cannon said eagerly, "Why don't we work together, Ray, instead of pulling against each other? Let's join forces. Our interests are identical."

Ray reached his decision. "Maybe I'm an awful sucker, but I'm going to play it your way. We've all got our necks stuck out a yard."

Jackie shuddered. "Oh, don't say that, please. It makes me think of..."

Ray grinned. He extended his hand across the table. The girl accepted it hesitantly. Cannon leaned across and laid his big hand on theirs. They looked like conspirators in agreement.

Ray said, "This changes my plans. Now I think maybe we ought to go back into the plant tonight, while things are still upset over there. It might give us a better chance to look through those files!"

Cannon's face twitched. "You and I could take the chance, Ray, but Jackie…"

"Jackie should go home," Ray said with conviction. "This job is not for a girl."

Jackie smiled wanly. "I suppose I should insist on going along with you two strong, silent, masterful men, but I won't. To tell the honest truth, what I saw tonight has got me down. So I think I'll take you up about going home."

Ray got up. "I'll phone for a taxi and while we're waiting"—he eyed the plate hungrily—"I'll finish these beans."

Later, as Ray and Cannon approached the entrance to the conduit tunnel, they could hear, from across the water, the rumble of skips on the inclines to the blast furnace loading bells and the shrilling of whistle signals from the rolling mills farther away. There was no lessening of the ceaseless clangor and roar of a great steel plant hurrying along its endless path of organized confusion.

Even though its guiding brain, in the person of Leonard Tracy, was dead, the plant possessed an impartial, soulless power of self-perpetuation. Already it answered to the direction of a new brain. And that new brain belonged to Quentin Harris.

Ray was in the lead. Sense of touch located for him the narrow tunnel opening with its shelf of lead-covered cables. One hand on the cables and the other against the concrete wall guided him as the passage dipped down beneath the water of the inlet.

Just as it leveled again, Ray came to an abrupt halt, holding a restraining hand against Cannon behind him. A rustling sound had come from the darkness straight ahead. Ray held his breath to listen.

There was nothing more. For a full two minutes he waited, ears straining. The tomblike silence was almost palpable, as was the smothering blackness.

His imagination stirred disquietingly. He remembered a trip he had once taken into the Endless Caverns in the Shenandoah Valley of Virginia. He recalled how, at a point two miles from the cave's mouth, the guide had extinguished all lights to show what total darkness was like. It had been no darker beneath Massanutten Mountain than it was now in this cable conduit under Ironton Inlet.

A sudden urgency seized Ray to get through, into fresh air again. Tugging at Cannon's sleeve, Ray hurried forward. His groping fingers touched something soft and yielding, something that slid away from him. An involuntary yell burst from his throat.

Then suddenly from the dead blackness ahead, a flashlight beam held them spotlighted.

THIRTEEN

The blinding beam prevented recognition of the person behind it, but the shadowy figure suddenly spoke. Ray recognized the deep, confident tone of Ulysses G. Flint.

"Locke!" the General exclaimed. "You scurvy scoundrel! Who's that with you?"

Ray felt a swift surge of returning confidence. "This," he said quietly, "is Glenn Cannon, Mr. Flint. I told you I saw Glenn in the plant. Since you've located this tunnel, you know how he managed to get in and out without passing through the gates. Incidentally, sir, how did *you* find the tunnel?"

"By studying detailed maps of the plant," the General said. "Obviously there was some means other than the gates whereby you were able to disappear as you did under Bixler's nose. Now tell me why you ran away, Locke. This is serious. You're even more deeply involved in Tracy's death than you were in Walter Keene's."

The big man stood blocking the narrow passage, with his light in the faces of both men blinding them, until Ray had told the detailed story of his race against Bixler's gun.

"What have you got to say about all this?" he demanded of Cannon.

Cannon replied unhesitatingly, "Ray's told you the truth. I had just discovered Tracy when Ray busted in on me. Naturally, I was scared. Didn't want anyone to know I was around where I had no business to be, particularly since murder had been committed."

To Ray, Flint said, "I suspected Bixler's yarn was fishy. He swore he caught you in the very act of sticking Tracy's head under the shear blades. Viewed in the light of information I've dredged up recently, it didn't quite ring true to me." There was satisfaction in his tone.

Abruptly, he questioned Cannon again. "Locke says you were at the laboratory the night Walter Keene was killed. Were you?"

"Yes."

"Did you kill Keene?"

"No."

"If you did, of course, you wouldn't admit it. What were you doing at the laboratory?"

"I intended to look through the storage files, to find the records of the tests on that axle. That was the test that sent me to jail, along with Ray."

"Why did you want to find it?"

"I'm sure it was faked. If I could prove any tests faked around this plant, I could establish my own innocence."

"You have an idea how such a thing could be done?"

"Certainly."

"I want to know about that." The General switched his flashlight out of their eyes and along the upward slant of the narrow concrete slot. "But let's get out of here. This is hardly the appropriate place for a council of war."

With the brilliant beam no longer blinding him, and with its radiance diffused by reflection from concrete surfaces, Ray could now see that the big bald-headed man had come into the tunnel wearing an impeccably tailored business suit. Yet, the grime and accumulated soot and dust of the subterranean passage had not so much as smudged the white cuffs of Flint's shirt.

Ray noted the dirt and grease on Glenn Cannon's work shirt and his own soiled and rumpled clothing. He and Cannon must have done a good job as human brooms in sweeping out the conduit tunnel, unless U. G. Flint were one of those incredible persons who could fall into a tar barrel and emerge clutching a bouquet of American Beauty roses.

When they reached the room which housed the transformers, the General turned off his light, went to the door, and looked around outside.

"We aren't likely to be interrupted for a while," he said when he returned. "Now, Cannon, I want something definite from you about these crooked tests."

Cannon gave a short, harsh laugh. "If I knew anything definite do you think I'd have served a year in stir?"

"I don't mean that. What I'm trying to do is find the party or parties responsible. You must have fairly specific ideas along those lines."

Cannon said, "The jury had very specific ideas. They said *I* was responsible."

"I know that, of course." The General was patient. "If I didn't think there were more to it than that, I wouldn't be wasting time with you. But falsification of tests did not cease when you left Ironton, Cannon. There have been other cases within the past few months. In fact, they are becoming more and more frequent."

"Yes, I know," Cannon admitted. "Jackie told me."

"Jackie? Oh, yes, you mean Miss North. Speaking of her, Cannon, what connection has she with all this?"

Ray answered. "She's his cousin, sir." He went on to tell the General how he had run into Cannon and the girl by chance at the cheap beanery.

The General said, "Now let's get back to these crooked tests. I know certain things about them already. I know, for instance, that this man Keene had deliberately falsified certain chemical analyses. But a chemist wouldn't be able to rig the physical tests."

Cannon said, "You're right on that. Whoever did it must have been someone with a certain authority around the physical lab. That means, either Ashley, Gaylord or myself."

"Leave yourself out of it!" Flint ordered. "We've heard your story, and Locke's. The fact that phony tests have still persisted lends credence to what you've both told me."

"All right. Then Ashley or Gaylord must have a hand in it."

"Which do you think?"

"Well, Ashley's job is largely administrative and along research lines. The practical everyday inspection work comes under jurisdiction of the Chief Inspector."

"So you think Gaylord is the lad we're after?"

Cannon hesitated. "I wouldn't want to condemn any man without proof. But as my assistant, Gaylord would have had ample opportunity for rigging the tests. And since he inherited my job, his chances certainly haven't decreased."

"Could he fake these tests all by himself?"

"Only to a limited extent. In pulling tensile tests, for instance, it's an old gag to run the machine too fast. In that way you can over-balance the arm of the scale and the reading is way too high. But such tests are pulled in the presence of the buyer's inspector. You couldn't work a mossy stunt like that on anyone but a green inspector."

"How about it, Locke?" the General asked. "Do you recall how fast the machine was run when you pulled those axle tests?"

"I wouldn't be likely to forget. I've pulled them again in my nightmares for the last year. The machine didn't go more than an eighth of an inch a minute, which is the specified maximum crosshead speed."

Cannon said, "On the axle tests, chances are there was a substitution of test pieces."

"How could that be done? I understand from Locke that the test specimens were marked by the inspector with his own private identification."

"That's correct, sir," Ray said. "But on those particular axles, specimens were hollow bored before submission to me. I was told it had been done to save time. Of course I didn't have to stamp the spots they'd selected for me, but I did it to cooperate."

The General said, "I don't understand. What do you mean they'd already been hollow bored?"

"The railroad inspector," Ray explained, "puts his stamp on a prolongation left in a certain percentage of the forgings for that purpose. He picks a spot halfway between the center of the forging and the outer surface and marks it there. The forging is then sent to the machine shop and a round piece of metal, large enough to be machined into a standard test piece, is hollow bored. It's as if you cut a cylinder from a tub of butter with a tin can. The cylinder is then broken from the casting and turned up on a lathe and sent to the lab for pulling the test."

"I still don't see how…"

In the complete darkness the voices of the three men produced an eerie effect, like disembodied spirits conversing in a graveyard at midnight.

"The way I doped it out, it could go like this," Ray said. "Suppose they have some axle forgings which they know won't meet requirements. They could cut a cylinder, or a core as it's properly called, from metal they know will pass the tests. Then they go ahead and hollow bore the forging, break out the core and throw it away. Next they thread the phony core, tap threads into the bottom of the hole in the forging and screw in the phony core. The inspector can't tell he hasn't a solid piece of the axle for his test." He appealed to Cannon. "Couldn't it be done like that?"

Cannon said, "Not only could, but has been, more than once by crooked steel men. I never allowed such things to be done at Ironton, but someone must have worked behind my back."

There was silence for a moment as the General thought it over. "I begin to see what you mean," he said.

"The inspector is really in a jam," Ray broke in eagerly. "If he won't approve the piece that's been already bored for him, he's afraid he will make a heel of himself. If he does…well, you know what happened to me!"

"Of course, the trick is to do a sales job on the inspector," Cannon added. "Give him a line about saving time, the way it was given Ray. And, of course, the inspector isn't dreaming that anyone would go to so much trouble to fool him—not unless he's been burnt before!"

"I should think," the General suggested, "that the threads on the fake core would show when the piece is broken out."

Cannon said, "That's taken care of by cutting part way through the core just above the threads so that it breaks in the weakest place. If it's cleverly done no one would ever suspect."

"Hmmm. It must be worth a lot to someone to have those forgings accepted."

"It is," Cannon said shortly. "Those guys in the forge shop are paid on a tonnage basis. Rejected material doesn't count."

"Who took you out to pick those tests?" Flint asked Ray. "Was it Gaylord?"

"No, sir. I just went into the hammer shop and some of the men there showed me the forgings."

"Quite likely the guy who went with Ray knew nothing about the phony business," Cannon added.

"Someone in the forge shop would have to be involved," the General said. He wasn't asking a question, he was speaking as if to himself.

Cannon said, "Someone in the forge shop would be the guy who paid off. He'd make it worthwhile for the plant inspector and then they'd have to get a machinist to do the boring and threading jobs for them."

"That would be the forge shop foreman, Al Sisco," U. G. Flint said with satisfaction. "Was he here in your time, Cannon?"

Both Ray and Glenn Cannon answered at the same time. "Yes, sir."

"Good. I've already ordered an investigation of him and also the machinist, Pete Kosleck."

The silence this time lasted for several minutes. Ray shifted uneasily in the darkness. Finally Flint said, "What do you intend to do about it, Cannon?"

"I've been trying to get at the records in the department files."

"You had somewhat the same idea, Locke."

"Yes, sir."

"Well, you're both wrong!" the General said abruptly. "You'll get nowhere fast. Already you've done more harm than good."

"But I've got to do something, sir. I can't just—"

"There's only one right way to clear the two of you," Flint said. "We've got to catch the guilty parties in the act."

"Easier said than done."

"Maybe so," Flint admitted. "But I've found there's a big order of carbon vanadium axles readying for the Gulf Southeastern within the next few days. Maybe there'll be some skullduggery in that connection."

"Why, that's the lot I heard Gaylord talking about the night of Keene's death," Ray exclaimed. "It was what he said about hollow boring them to save time that gave me the first confirmation of the trick we've been talking about. I'll bet there's something wrong going on with that lot."

"Could be," Cannon admitted. "What do you want me to do?"

"I want you to do exactly nothing!" the General snapped. "Leave everything to me. The best thing you can possibly do is to go back through this tunnel and stay away from Ironton until I send for you."

"But—"

"Don't argue!" The General's tone had become sharp. "Just do as I say. Your presence in or around this plant will only complicate matters. Don't you see that I'm duty-bound to turn you over to the police in connection with Tracy's murder?"

Ray said, "What about me, sir?"

"I might need your help, Locke, although you're rather deeply involved in the Tracy matter, also."

"But you don't think that I—"

The General said, "We've already gone all over that ground. Let's not repeat."

"But what do you think about Tracy, Mr. Flint? You must suspect someone."

"Everybody and his grandmother was around at the time Tracy was killed," said Ulysses Flint. "And there are motives galore for them all. Most of the motives tie in with the crookedness in the Test Department. Take your choice—Gaylord or Ashley, or the smaller fry, Sisco or Kosleck."

"You're counting out Clara Dunne?"

"A very interesting thing about Miss Dunne," the General said. "She has been greatly upset over Leonard Tracy's death. It appears now that she and Tracy were secretly engaged to be married. She says they'd kept it quiet but just yesterday afternoon they'd settled the date and were getting ready to announce it."

"He was in Clara's office at least twice earlier today," Ray said thoughtfully. "And they both looked pretty serious."

"It would be instructive," the General went on, "if we could know what your friend Bixler was doing so close to the place of Tracy's death. Obviously, the man did a considerable amount of dirty work for his big boss."

"And how about Harris?" Ray could not refrain from asking. "He's the one who stands to gain most from having Tracy out of the way. He'll be General Super. The difference in salary between the two jobs must amount to twenty thousand a year. And Tracy told me he and Harris didn't get on at all well."

"We shall certainly have to remember Quentin Harris," the General's voice purred smoothly from the darkness. "But there are two other principal suspects we must not forget, either."

"Who are they?"

"Ray Locke and Glenn Cannon. Both were at the scene of the crime. Both might have had excellent motives. Cannon believed he was unjustly treated. Locke thought Tracy might have designs on his life. Both had served prison terms in connection with falsified tests."

Ray caught his breath. "But I thought you said you didn't...."

"I know who the murderer is," U. G. Flint said very softly.

"You know! Then why..."

"I can't prove it," the General said. "But I know because the murderer left a calling card with each victim."

"A calling card!"

"Call it an identifying mark, if you prefer. You remember the mark on Keene's head?"

"The swage mark?"

"No. The other. The smaller semi-circle, like a half moon."

"Yes, sir. I remember that."

"There was a similar mark on Tracy's head," the General said. "To my mind it's conclusive proof of the killer's identity."

"Then why don't you turn him in to the police?"

"I said I could prove nothing yet. I want to give the criminal plenty of rope—rope for the hangman. That, Locke, is where I'm going to need your help."

"Whatever you say, Mr. Flint."

"Finding who is responsible for these murders is just part of my plan," the General went on. "My more important task is to clear up this matter of crookedness at Ironton once and for all. The good name of American-Consolidated Steel is of considerable more moment than the death of one or two persons, even if one of them did happen to be the big boss at Ironton."

There was another short silence while both Ray and Cannon waited for the General's next words.

"I shall not be ready for final action," the General said, "until I have word from certain confidential bank connections in New York. There are still aspects of this case which I don't understand at all. But I shall make it a point to look at the Gulf Southeastern forgings tonight."

The bald streak on Ulysses Flint's head shone in the light of the flash as the big man inspected his platinum wrist watch briefly.

"It is now a quarter to eleven," the General said, as he switched the light off again. "I want you, Locke, to meet me at that checker-work place at precisely one o'clock. You, Cannon, will go back through the tunnel and stay away from the Ironton Works as I previously suggested. Let me have an address or phone where I can reach you and I will see that you are informed as soon as there is any progress to report."

"How do I know you don't intend to double-cross me?" Cannon demanded without finesse.

"You don't." The General's voice was serene. "That's the chance you have to take. But if you *don't* take it, chances are you'll find yourself up to the ears in trouble."

"All right." Cannon sounded sullen. "I guess I have no choice. You can phone me at Madison 3-2784."

The General held his light again while he jotted the numbers in a small black memo hook. Then, "Get along," he said. "Locke, you can walk with me halfway back toward the mills."

FOURTEEN

Ray could imagine how the actual murderer must feel. Instinctively he shrank from light, as a nocturnal animal shrinks from his cave mouth at midday. He felt a sense of isolation, of being set apart from his fellow man, accentuated by the fact that he had to be careful to avoid anyone who might recognize him and raise an alarm.

His task was an easier one than that of the murderer, however, Ray reasoned. The inner tension must be less. The only thing required of him was physical alertness, whereas the real killer had his conscience to combat.

An hour and a half had passed since he had left the General near the elevated trestles on the approach to the merchant mills. An hour and a half, during which Ray had skulked in shadows, one eye always on the large clock over the plant's main gate. Never had an hour and a half seemed so endlessly long.

He struck out now for the more congested area of the Ironton Works. He would go the long way around, he decided. It would help kill the remaining half hour. Actual danger was slight. The night was dark. With his hat brim pulled down well over his forehead, chances of his being recognized were remote.

He encountered men occasionally in the spaces between mill buildings. Ray walked briskly, as if on a purpose connected with his work. No one gave him a second glance. He avoided the spots where the lights were brightest, plodding ahead steadily with lowered head.

The Open Hearth loomed monstrous against the blackness of the sky, red glow spilling from its ports as from the open firebox of a locomotive. Above the lighted arches, dark building walls faded quickly, vanishing completely into the obscurity of night.

It now lacked but a minute or so until one o'clock. Ray hurried on to the end of the long structure, confidently expecting to find the General waiting at the door to the checker-work chamber. But when he reached the building end, Ulysses G. Flint was not there.

Ray waited, fidgeting impatiently. The nervousness against which he had been fighting grew as minutes lengthened. Suppose the General did not show up at all? Ray began to realize how completely all his hopes and his future were dependent upon the big, scrubby-mustached man, and how little he actually knew of what went on inside the General's head.

The delay was becoming unbearable. Ray went to the iron door. He struck a match. The door was locked. A new padlock had been substituted for one he had broken.

He walked a few steps to the end of the building, came back again, pacing restlessly. As be passed the door to the checker-work chambers the third time, he thought he heard a sound.

He stopped to listen. Something was moving behind the padlocked entrance.

He moved close again. The door rattled. It sounded as if someone were knocking against it, weakly, from the inside. Then Ray noted the faint edge of light which showed at the sides and bottom of the door.

Someone was inside...padlocked in!

Quickly Ray ran around the end of the building and up the stairs to the charging floor of the Open Hearth. He found a sledge where he had found one before, near the side of Number Eleven furnace; he brought it down with him, smashed the padlock with a well-aimed blow.

Light struck out at him as he flung open the iron door—light and heat. The checker-work chamber, cool before, was now like an oven.

At his feet, electric light shone on the body of a man. Ulysses Flint lay just inside the door.

Ray's first thought was that the General was dead. But suddenly the big man's black eyes flew open, he grunted, tried to sit up. Ray knelt swiftly at Flint's side, helped him to an upright position.

"What happened?" he asked anxiously. "Are you badly hurt, sir?"

The General grunted again. He passed his hand across his head, wheezed, climbed to his feet with a big paw on Ray's shoulder to steady himself.

"No—not seriously hurt. A bit—shaky."

"But what..."

The General's neat gray suit was soiled now, the white of his shirt grimed by contact with the dirty masonry underfoot. He made an instinctive gesture as if to regain his former spotlessness by dusting himself with his hands. Then he lurched toward the door.

"It's stifling, let's get out of here."

Cooler air from outside was sweeping through the iron door, but Ray wiped sweat from his face as he followed the General outside. It was like coming from the steam room of a Turkish bath.

"I was slugged," the General explained. He stood with his feet spread wide apart as if to brace himself.

The big man fingered his head again, tenderly, then bent so that light from the open door fell squarely upon it. "Take a look and tell me what this is, Locke." Ray moved to see better. Outlined against the smooth shininess of the man's bald streak the General's blunt forefinger indicated a crescent-shaped red mark a trifle smaller than a dime.

"It's like the bruise on Walter Keene's head," Ray told U. G. Flint.

"And on Leonard Tracy's." There was an odd note of satisfaction in the General's tone. "Just as I thought. The same person who killed Keene and Tracy has made an attempt on my own life. That, Locke, is the mark of the murderer."

Eagerly, Ray asked, "Who is it, Mr. Flint?"

"For excellent reasons of my own, I'm not going to answer that question just yet." The General had completely recovered his self-assurance. "If I did, I might never be able to prove it. We made one bad mistake already in underestimating the intelligence and cunning of the killer. It was a close squeak. I can't afford another mistake."

"You haven't yet told me what happened," Ray reminded.

"I knew there was danger, of course," the General said. "Therefore, I took the precaution of fastening myself into that room with a new padlock on the inside so I couldn't be surprised. But the murderer must have been hidden in the inner room when I came in. I was poking around the work bench when I was hit from behind. The murderer then turned the valve so that flames from the adjoining checker-work would roast or suffocate me."

"It's a miracle you escaped!" Ray exclaimed feelingly. He felt a selfish wonder as to what might have happened to Ray Locke if the only person who believed in his innocence had been violently eliminated.

"My head must he thicker than I believed," said Ulysses Flint. His broad features twisted into a grin more human than any expression Ray had seen him wear before. "I was stunned, but I regained my senses quickly enough to turn the valve and shut off the flame. The murderer had switched off the lights, taken the padlock key from my pocket, and locked me in. I turned the lights back on. Thought you might see them around the door sills. If you hadn't come when you did..."

He shrugged expressively.

"How long ago did this all happen?" Ray tingled with sudden renewed excitement.

"I must have been out ten or fifteen minutes," the General said. "About half an hour ago, I should say."

That was ample time for anyone to have gone from the Open Hearth to almost any other portion of the steel works.

The General fumbled in his breast pocket, located his cigar case and selected a thick Perfecto. Not till he had bitten the end from the cigar and had it comfortably aglow, did he make further comment.

"I come to the regretful conclusion," he observed then, "that our personnel at Ironton includes a bunch of crooks and murderers. Test records at the laboratory are not all that have surreptitiously been removed, Locke. Those drawings of the fixation plants at Rjukan and Notodden have vanished also—taken by the murderer, without a doubt. This matter of nitrogen plays an ever increasingly important part in the whole case."

The end of the big man s cigar brightened as the General puffed vigorously. "We've work to do," he said briskly. "I've made inquiries, Locke, and I find that the Gulf Southeastern inspector will be at Ironton to get his locomotive axles tomorrow morning. You and I, therefore, are going to pay a surprise visit to the forge tonight."

The hammer shop was even more cavernous, gloomier than in daytime. The open forges no longer gleamed along the walls; no glowing metallic ice cast streamers of flame and smoke beneath the heat of the monster steam hammers. Unlike actual steel-making processes, such as the blast furnaces, the Bessemer and the Open Hearth, the forge shop did not operate twenty-four hours a day.

In the central portion of the structure, yellow light streamed down from flood lamps located up by the roof trusses. A traveling crane was moving billets to the side of a four-ton hammer. The crane operator, arms crossed on the side of his cage, looked down at the small group of men working beneath him.

The two ends of the building where no work was going on were in comparative obscurity. But the General, who seemed to have some definite plan in mind, went directly to the idle hammer next to the one where Walter Keene had been killed. He reached for a long electric cord hanging from the roof, switched on a two-hundred-watt bulb.

"Now, Locke," he said, "this is your opportunity to do something constructive about your own problem. From what you and your friend Cannon told me tonight of the possible *modus operandi* employed in the falsification of axle tests, we have at least a chance of getting positive evidence."

"What do you wish me to do, Mr. Flint?"

"You're familiar with the test procedure. I get the general drift of your remarks, but I want you to show me, if you can, how these specimens are prepared, and whether or not there is anything crooked about this material for the Gulf Southeastern."

Ray moved to the side of the billet pile. "Here, sir," he said and his heart was thumping suddenly with almost painful excitement. "These have all been hollow bored *prior to inspection*—the same as that un-lucky test I pulled myself."

He indicated a spot on the end of a billet, halfway between center and outside of the forging. A circular hole, some two inches in diameter had been bored into the metal in a direction parallel to the length of the forging. In the center of this hole, like a miniature tree stump rising from a miniature well, was a solid core of metal.

"You see," Ray explained, "the inspector puts his hammer stamp on the end of the core. Then they break it out with a maul and a wedge and take it over to the machine shop to be turned into the standard test specimen."

"So if the core is actually a phony…"

"We can unscrew it. Yes, sir."

Ray looked around rapidly, found a pair of leather-palmed work gloves on the anvil underneath the steam hammer. He drew them on.

At this moment a gruff voice called from behind them. "Hey, you!"

Ray and the General turned at the same moment. The hammer shop foreman, Al Sisco, was coming toward them, threading his way swiftly around the billet piles.

"Why, you're the same guys what was hangin' around here the other day," he exclaimed with apparent surprise. An angry red, visible even be-neath the sweat-streaked soot which grimed the man's features, colored his heavy face and thick neck. "I told ya then to get outta here!"

"And I told you I'm here by authority of the plant management," the General said grimly. "Don't bother us. We're busy." To Ray he added, "Go ahead, Locke."

Ray seized the metal core of the hollow-bored forging. He twisted it vigorously.

Sisco roared, "If you don't get outta here I'm gonna bust ya one. You can't come into my shop an'…"

He came at Ray as he spoke. The General took a quick step forward, intercepting the burly foreman's rush. One big hand shot out and seized Sisco's wrist. The other hand clamped down instantly behind it. The General pivoted. He caught Sisco's forward momentum against his hip, jerking upward at the same instant.

Sisco shot into the air. His heels described a complete arc over his head. He landed flat on his back with a solid thump on the dirt floor, nar-rowly missing the end of the billet pile. The breath burst from his lungs in a grunting *whoosh.*

For a hare instant Sisco lay motionless. Then he scrambled to his feet. His dirty face was contorted with rage and surprise. "Why you god-damn—"

"Don't say it!" the General warned. His voice was quiet but deadly. "And don't start anything, Sisco. You might be badly hurt."

Ulysses Flint was a big man. But the hammer shop foreman was bigger—a veritable giant, with a wrist thick as an average man's biceps and arms toughened by years of labor at the forge.

"Hurt!" Sisco bellowed. "Goddamn it, I'm gonna *kill* ya!"

He rushed at the General with arms flailing. There was nothing scientific about his attack; it was the frenzied drive of an angry hull.

Ulysses Flint sidestepped. For such a big man he was amazingly light-footed. Little swirls of dust spiraled up through the stark glare of the bright electric light as his feet moved in a quick pattern. To Ray, crouching open-mouthed beside the billet pile, it seemed as if he were placing them in orderly sequence on invisibly numbered squares.

As Sisco's rush carried him past, the General lashed out suddenly. He did not strike with his fist, but with the edge of his hand as in jiu-jitsu. The shop foreman staggered, threw up both his grimy hands to his face as if he had been hit with an axe. When he turned he was panting, bubbles of saliva drooling from the comers of his mouth.

The General's voice cracked sharply. "I'm warning you for the last time, Sisco!"

But Sisco was beyond warning. He gathered himself together again, shaking with fury. When he lunged, his brawny arms were spread wide as if he would scoop in his opponent to crush him in an infuriated bear-grip.

Ray, watching, thought the General's footwork beautiful to behold. Flint eluded the giant's rush entirely. This time he struck with his right fist and with all the weight of his powerful body behind it. It landed right behind the ear, with a flat sound like a baseball smacking into a catcher's mitt.

Sisco's knees buckled. He went down as if he'd been shot, his grimy face plowing a furrow in the dry dust of the shop floor.

Ulysses Flint stepped back and slapped his hands together as if he were brushing away an unpleasant contamination. There wasn't a drop of perspiration or a speck of dirt on the man's face, other than what he had picked up previously from the floor of the checker-work chamber. He was not even breathing heavily.

"Had me worried," he confided to Ray. "It's dreadfully simple to kill a man. Why, one time down in Laredo…" He stopped abruptly. "A blow with the side of the hand can break a human neck easier than you'd realize," he finished lamely after a moment.

Sisco sat up in the dirt. There was no more fight left in the shop foreman.

The General stood with a wary eye on Sisco, but it was Ray to whom he was speaking. "Go ahead," he ordered. "We've got a job to do."

Ray twisted the core of the hollow-bored billet. It remained unmoved. He exerted all his strength. Still nothing happened.

"Looks like a false alarm," he said finally, after several more efforts. His pale face mirrored deep disappointment.

The General's expression was unchanged. "Anyhow, we tried," he said.

A mocking smile had spread over Sisco's dirt-encrusted features. "You guys ain't so damn' smart," he muttered.

"Wait a minute," Ray said. He was examining the black collar of the axle forging, upon which the identification numbers had been stamped. "There may be more than one heat involved in such a big batch of forgings."

He moved around the billet pile, peering at each one, lips moving as he murmured the heat number under his breath.

"I was right, sir," he said at last. "Here's one from another heat."

He stooped again, twisting with his gloved hand at the core in the billet prolongation.

"This is it!" he shouted suddenly in wild excitement. "See!"

Ulysses Flint stepped over to get a better look. The core was moving in Ray's grip. In another moment he had it out, stood up, holding the core for Flint to see.

The end of the core, previously invisible, had been machined to a smooth, smaller diameter into which threads were cut. Just above the first turn of the threads, a small nick entirely circled the metal.

"That's where it's supposed to break," Ray pointed. "The inspector wouldn't notice the small edge where it's been cut. He'd take a quick look at the fracture and, of course, he wouldn't see the piece again until it came back from the machine shop."

Sisco's grin had turned into a black scowl, as the General faced him again.

"I guess that winds up the game as far as *you're* concerned," Flint said. "No wonder you were so full of fight. It'll go easier with you now if you tell me who else was in on this with you."

Sisco muttered, "I ain't no squealer."

The General shrugged. "Suit yourself. I gave you one piece of advice you didn't take. Now I'm going to give you another. Take it or leave it. But if you think the only thing involved is a hit of chiseling against some big railroad, you're sadly mistaken. Unless you come clean right now and spill everything you know, you're facing a murder rap, Sisco—*two* murder raps! I'm going to see that you're formally charged with the slaying of Walter Keene and—"

"I didn't kill nobody!"

"Keene was killed under that very hammer." The General jerked his thumb to the ten-thousand-pound behemoth adjoining. "It takes skill to operate one of those things, Sisco. And it takes a lot of skill to crack a man's skull without beating his whole head to a pulp. Just anyone couldn't do it. But you could."

"Honest to Gawd!"

"We're wasting time," the General said briskly. "Where's your telephone, Sisco? I'm going to call the Iron and Steel Police."

The shop foreman turned defiant again. "If ya aim to phone, s'pose ya find it yerself!"

"No. You're going to show me." Flint walked over beside the sullen man. Before Sisco knew what he intended, the General had seized his arm again, twisting it swiftly behind his back in an arm lock. "Now march, Sisco! Before I have to break your arm."

Sisco marched.

"You call," the General told Ray. "I seem to have my hands full." His smile was ironic. "Ask to speak with the Chief—with Bixler. Tell him to get over here right away."

The company cop's voice came over the wire.

Ray was thoroughly enjoying himself. "This is Ray Locke," he said into the mouthpiece, speaking very distinctly. "I'm over at the forge shop now, if you care to see me."

He held the receiver away from his ear as it suddenly began to crackle violently. Then, "Cut out the horsing around, Bixler," he ordered roughly. "Mr. U. G. Flint wants you over here and he says to make it snappy. He can't he waiting around all night for a lug like you."

He pronged the receiver, grinning.

"Now, Sisco," the General said, "are you talking or do you want your neck in a sling?"

Sisco cracked. "I didn't do nothin'. I rigged some tests for them inspectors, sure. That ain't no crime."

"Who helped you fake the tests?"

"There wasn't nobody."

"In that case you're the only one with a murder motive."

"Ben Gaylord knew about it," Sisco said hurriedly. "In this shop they pay a tonnage bonus. I cut Ben in on the gravy."

"And someone in the machine shop—Pete Kosleck, for instance?"

Sisco nodded glumly.

"Did anyone else in the Test Department know about this? Mr. Ashley, for instance?"

"I don't know." The foreman's words rang true. "Ben Gaylord fixed everything. He's the only guy I paid off."

The General rubbed his hands with satisfaction. "The murderer's whole rotten fabric commences to disintegrate. Meanwhile the company's dirty linen emerges in pristine whiteness."

* * * *

He and Ray Locke stood together at the forge shop entrance. A loud and profane Bixler had arrived belligerently only to depart with his fires neatly and efficiently quenched. With Bixler had gone the equally subdued Al Sisco.

"I don't know how to thank you, Mr. Flint," Ray began. "It looks as though I may be cleared after all."

"Thank me!" the General snorted. "You don't need to worry about thanks, Locke, not after what happened at the Open Hearth tonight. I've been using you, that's all. I needed your technical knowledge. Lambert and his boys would have been like fish out of water on a thing like this. And, now, Locke…"

"Yes, sir?"

"I'm going to need your help again—in rather a big way."

"Anything I can do, of course."

"I want you to get back to that tunnel and out of the plant. Bixler's seen you. I rather took his whiskers off a few minutes ago, but he may inform Lambert you're here. The police are looking for you, of course. I want to be able to tell Lambert truthfully that I don't know where you are."

Ray waited in silence for him to go on.

"Stay away from the Ironton Works until eight o'clock tomorrow night," U. G. Flint continued. "At eight o'clock, I want you to be downstairs in the Test Department building. I will see to it that there are test pieces to be pulled in the big machine. You will go into the lab, take the test pieces and break them in the machine, in the usual way. Got that clear?"

"Yes, sir. But what…"

"That's all you have to do," the General said. "Just leave the rest to me. I have a very definite reason for everything."

"Will you be at the laboratory, Mr. Flint?"

"No one but yourself will be there at eight o'clock," Ulysses Flint said positively. "But someone wall come in shortly after you arrive. That person will be the murderer, Locke. I will need you to tell me who he is."

"What shall I do when he comes in?"

"Nothing. Just go about your business. You will be in no personal danger, that I promise you."

Ray hesitated. "Is that all?"

"That's all. I think I can safely say that if you follow my instructions to the letter, you will find yourself vindicated completely before tomorrow night is over." The big man made a pushing motion with his hand. "Get along now!"

As Ray was about to stride off into the plant, the General put a restraining hand on his arm. "Better check your watch now, Locke. I don't want you to be late."

Ray flushed, and admitted that he had pawned his wrist watch.

The General swiftly unfastened his own watch from his wrist, handed it to Ray. "Here, take this, son. Time is more important than you realize now. Remember, be there at eight o'clock on the dot—no sooner and no later."

"I'll be there, sir," Ray promised.

FIFTEEN

In accordance with his previous intent, Ray sought sanctuary across the inlet. Traffic through the tunnel, he thought with grim humor, was becoming comparable to that of the Hudson Tubes.

Around the tapping hole, or iron notch, of an abandoned furnace, he found that time and the weather had deeply eroded the steel outer shell. Inside, the firebrick lining had also disintegrated. The hole, normally but eight inches square, was now large enough so that he could readily crawl through. Inside, he had a private fortress.

He stayed there until the next evening. Obeying the General's instructions to the letter, he reached the Test Department building precisely at eight. There was a light upstairs where the night chemist was on duty. As usual, the gooseneck above the entrance at the side corridor by Ashley's office was glaring. But the building downstairs was completely dark.

Taut as a compressed spring, Ray went in through the outer room, switching on lights as he did so. He had the uncomfortable feeling that eyes were watching him from the dark as he passed into the physical lab.

Quickly he flipped switches until the big room was lighted like a Christmas tree.

As the General had promised, a pile of neatly machined test specimens was waiting for him on the table near the big Norton machine. Ray got a ruled sheet of report paper and a pencil and put them on the table beside the specimens.

He picked up one of the specimens from the pile, a smooth steel shaft about six inches long and half an inch in diameter, turned to hourglass shape in the middle and with screw threads cut at each end to fit the testing machine.

The Norton machine was a tall, black affair which looked like some kind of press. It had a long arm at the right, like a weighing scale. Ray pulled a switch to start the motor.

The lab filled with a steady droning sound. Ray cast an involuntary glance about him, searching the shadows along the wall as if the murderer were lurking there, ready to pounce upon him.

With an effort of will, he turned back to the machine. He shifted a lever and the crosshead moved rapidly upward. He measured the diameter of the test specimen at its narrowest point, using a micrometer caliper.

When he started to enter the figures upon the report sheet he realized that he had forgotten them. Pulling himself together impatiently, Ray measured it again and jotted the result upon the paper.

He shifted the lever once more and, as the crosshead ceased to move, inserted the test specimen between the jaws of the machine. He threw the worm gear which controlled the machine into slow downward motion. The jaws moved gradually apart again.

As they did so, Ray cranked a movable weight along the scale arm, keeping the arm in balance as the tension on the test specimen increased. Suddenly, the scale arm dropped.

The sharp smack of metal against metal made Ray jump. Once more he cast a furtive glance over his shoulder. No one was visible in the room except himself.

He entered the scale reading on his record as the motor continued to drone. The scale arm jerked up again.

Ray cranked the weight farther along the scale. When the test piece broke in its middle section, the dull *thump* made him jump for the second time.

His nervousness made him furious at himself. He took the broken fragments from the machine, examined the fracture briefly, tossed them into the scrap pile.

He entered the scale reading and the fracture appearance on the record. Then, shifting the lever so the crosshead moved rapidly upward again, he reached for the next test piece.

A muffled rustling sound reached his ears from somewhere behind the machine, followed by a faint, high-pitched squeak.

Keyed up as he was, his muscles almost refused to function. He stood with the test piece still in his fingers, frozen into immobility, while imagination painted lurid pictures of the murderer creeping upon him with the weapon which left a crescent-shaped bruise.

Suddenly he realized that his tense, strained appearance might warn the murderer. Evidently Ulysses Flint had not expected him to indicate in any way that the culprit was in danger of exposure.

Gently he set the test specimen back upon the table. The stealthy noise, which came again, seemed to originate from a tall metal container near the wall back of the Norton machine. Warily Ray circled the scale arm to investigate. He took one look into the container, then laughed aloud. The can was half filled with clean cotton waste. On this soft bedding, the laboratory cat, Oscar, had made himself comfortable…along with five, tiny newborn kittens. Oscar, it seemed, had recently become a mother!

The cat blinked up at Ray, rumbling with a deep purr as Ray's head appeared above the top of the big can. One of the blind, helpless kittens, scrambling feebly among its brothers in search of nourishment, mewed loudly now, a piteous baby cry, as it nuzzled Oscar's warmth.

Ray went back to his test pieces. His chuckle held a more genuine note of amusement as he shifted the control lever and pulled the next tensile test.

Then a step sounded on the wooden floor of the outer room. Ray looked up quickly. One person, the General had said, would be coming to the physical lab tonight...

Benjamin Gaylord walked into the room.

The Chief Inspector was dressed for the street. His suit, a light shade of brown, was newer, less shabby than his customary clay-colored attire. He was sucking the stem of an empty pipe and his eyes, sunk deep into his bony skull, contemplated Ray with mild surprise.

"Didn't expect to find *you* here!" he remarked with open curiosity. "Where've you been, Ray? You're supposed to have run out after killing Tracy, y'know."

Ray said, "I know. But I had nothing to do with Tracy."

He was surprised at his complete lack of nerves, now that he was actually face to face with the skulking killer. Even with the knowledge that Gaylord had been his own logical choice for the murderer, it was hard for Ray to picture the man as deadly; difficult to imagine the shabby, bony-faced Chief Inspector smashing a man's head beneath a steam hammer and guillotining another with the alligator shears.

But Ulysses Flint had been explicit. Only one man would come into the laboratory tonight—the murderer.

"I suppose I should notify the authorities that you're here. But I can't imagine you as the murderer of Leonard Tracy," Gaylord said. His friendly matter-of-fact tone added to Ray's sense of unreality. "I've got an appointment now, but I want to have a good long talk with you, Ray. Stick around, will you, until I'm free?"

Ray mumbled, "Sure."

He turned back to the test machine, keeping one eye on Gaylord as the man went past him to the stairs.

What now? he thought. The General had told him nothing, except to note who came to the lab. The indicated procedure then, was for him to continue with the test specimens.

Excitement had gripped him now. It was very hard to pay proper attention to the test machine. He clamped another specimen between the jaws and started it downward.

Something moving in the corridor beyond Ashley's office caught his eye. Had Gaylord come down again silently?

He turned just in time to see the dead-pan profile of Glenn Cannon as the man started up the stairs to the chemical lab. For all of Cannon's weight, he moved without a sound.

Ray was confused. The General had specified that there would be *one* visitor tonight. He had also positively ordered Cannon to stay away from the Ironton Works. Was Cannon then the murderer, and not Gaylord?

Scarcely had the question presented itself, when a third figure passed quietly through the corridor. This time it was a girl—Jackie North, right on Glenn Cannon's heels.

It was thoroughly bewildering. Undoubtedly something had gone wrong with the General's plan. Ray was sure of it when Ashley himself came in through the outer room.

The bearded Engineer of Tests looked Ray squarely in the face. There was something akin to hatred in the man's eyes. He opened his mouth as if to say something, thought better of it and went past without a word. Unlike Cannon, Ashley walked heavily; Ray could hear his feet on the stair treads going up.

Ashley had barely reached the upstairs before Ray heard the *tap-tap* of a woman's high heels coming down. It must he Jackie North again, he thought.

But it was Clara Dunne in her twill laboratory coat who reached the bottom of the steps. And just as she did so, the ugly face of "Windpipe" Bixler appeared through the side corridor.

He heard Bixler say, "Evenin', Miss Dunne." The company cop's tone was oily, ingratiating.

Clara Dunne brushed past the man. "Good evening," she said and her tone was very cool.

She was at Ashley's door as Bixler went up the stairs. Ray could hear her rattle the knob and mutter, "Darn! It's locked."

Clara turned and went back upstairs. Ray was completely at a loss to understand the sudden turn of events. Instead of there being but one person at the lab tonight, all of Ironton seemed to be milling around the test building.

It struck Ray suddenly that every suspect in the murder case was now here, with the sole exception of Quentin Harris. Could it be that the General had stated his expectation in exact reverse? Was it possible that the only person who did *not* come to the laboratory tonight would be the murderer?

But if that were the case, how did it happen that…

He heard a sound behind him, the barest whisper of sound. He whirled instantly. The lights in the physical lab went out as he did so.

Nothing was entirely clear after that, just impressions. He caught a glimpse of a wide, black bulk just behind him. Then he felt the crashing physical pain of a blow on the head.

After that, he had no sense of sight—just of feel.

He felt the rough floor boards smacking him suddenly in the face, strong arms dragging him upright, lifting him easily. He felt cold steel beneath his stomach as his attacker slid him between the vertical screws of the test machine.

Then his other senses began to return. He could identify the dry cottony taste of the waste stuffed roughly into his mouth, and hear the gears of the Norton machine being shifted.

The chill against his stomach was greater. It came now from within rather than from the cold metal on which he lay. Nightmare horror grew inside him, like a freezing ball just under his diaphragm.

Ray knew what would happen when the crosshead of the machine pinned him against the base. The testing machine could be used for compression tests as well as tensile, for crushing as well as tearing apart. It was strong enough to squeeze a two-inch cylinder of steel into a crumpled disk.

His brain was functioning again, except that there was a short circuit somewhere between the motor centers and its connecting nerves. His muscles would not obey instructions. It was as if he had been stricken with paralysis. He tried to shout, but his vocal cords were dead. In addition, the cottony waste in his mouth made an efficient gag.

He felt the slowly descending crosshead press against the small of his back. It tightened as the vertical screws of the machine turned at eighth-inch-a-minute speed. How long would it be, he wondered, before his spine would crack?

From the inward side of the laboratory door, a bulky figure moved. As Ray writhed with returning muscular strength, too late to avoid the tightening grip of the machine, the figure was silhouetted against the lighted square of the corridor door.

In profile, the rectangular, beefy form was easily recognizable.

It was Quentin Harris.

In the extremity of his terror and desperation, Ray had time for one bitter thought:

He had trusted Ulysses G. Flint. And Flint had betrayed him.

SIXTEEN

One more minute and it was over. Someone shouted. Lights came on, revealing the powerful presence of Ulysses G. Flint.

The General reached the Norton machine in one leap from his position by the wall switch. The pressure of the descending crosshead, just beginning to clamp painfully against Rays spine, relaxed instantly as Flint thrust the control lever upward into high speed.

Then the General was dragging Ray across the steel block, out from between the vertical screws. He plucked the wad of cotton waste from Ray's mouth.

Vaguely, Ray saw people swarming downstairs from the chemical lab, alarmed by the shouting and confusion. His knees were wobbly from shock and sudden relief. He brushed sweat from his forehead with the back of his hand.

"A few more minutes…" he said.

The General spoke sharply, "Nonsense, Locke! I *told* you there would be no personal danger. Have you no faith?"

Ray managed a feeble grin. "What's the quotation, sir, about faith being known through works?"

"You've suffered nothing more serious than a bad fright," the General insisted with complete lack of sympathy. "I knew you'd have a scare—a scare and a rap over the head. But with your assistance, our murder case is now, in the idiom of the day, 'busted wide open.'"

"I don't see," Ray began dazedly, "what I've done, except…"

"Naturally you don't." The General was brisk. He turned to the curious faces pressing behind. "Tonight," he said evenly, "I had planned a little round table conference in Mr. Tracy's former office. But someone, it appears, decided to alter my plans at the last minute. As it happens, that is quite satisfactory. We will hold the conference forthwith—here and now!"

Standing there near the balance arm of the test machine, the center of attention, the General was like a sales manager haranguing his staff. His dark eyes swept restlessly over the faces, tabulating them all mentally. It seemed as though he were weighing each individual in the scales of his mind and that no secrets would remain after that weighing was complete.

Ray ticked them all off his own mental list. They were all here, except the workmen, Sisco and Kosleck.

There was the wisp-bearded Ashley; the cadaver-like Gaylord; the plug-ugly Bixler; the dead-pan Glenn Cannon; and the women, Clara Dunne and Jackie North.

In the rear of the group Ray noticed the hatchet face of the homicide lieutenant, Lambert. Standing beside Lambert, Quentin Harris' pale eyes were fixed intently upon the General.

"All of you," the General said earnestly, "Have a vital stake in the reputation and good name of American-Consolidated Steel. That's why I want to say what I have to say in front of you all. I am trusting that your selfish interest, as well as your sense of obligation and responsibility, will prevent anything reflecting adversely upon the company from going any farther than this group. I feel that if you do not know the true facts, a basis for ugly and distorted rumors might be laid. But I do wish to emphasize that the crimes which have been committed in the Ironton Works have been the doings of individuals. In no sense do they reflect upon the company, or its management, or upon the steel industry."

U. G. Flint's eyes sought out Ashley among the intent group. His next words seemed to be addressed directly to the bearded Engineer of Tests.

"It will not come particularly as news to anyone present that there has been trouble in connection with falsified tests involving certain products manufactured at this plant. The matter first came to the attention of the company management, and to public notice as well, with resultant unfortunate publicity, when the streamliner, *Prairie Comet*, was wrecked slightly more than a year ago and a number of persons killed."

The General's eyes left Ashley and rested momentarily upon Glenn Cannon. "When Cannon and Locke were convicted and sent to prison, our people in New York thought the matter was ended. But they were wrong. Since that time, there have been indications of similar wrongdoing!"

Christopher Ashley shook his head violently. "I shall have to differ with you on that, Mr. Flint. I don't think…"

The General silenced the man with a lifted hand. "Wait, please! You will have your opportunity to talk. I repeat, then, evidence of further crookedness at Ironton was brought to the attention of the New York office. Very fortunately, no more fatal accidents have resulted and there has been no further damaging publicity. But New York was seriously alarmed. They requested me to investigate the situation. And so it was arranged that my very able friend, Mr. Quentin Harris, be sent from New York and placed in a position of sufficient responsibility so that he might get accurate first-hand knowledge of conditions at Ironton under the Tracy administration."

Ray drew in his breath sharply. What an idiot he had been not to realize why the General had never suspected Harris! It was so very obvious now that the two men had been working together from the start.

Ulysses Flint was continuing. "The management knew, of course, that the type of rascality involved might be exceedingly difficult to smoke out. While it might mean nothing more than one or two weak sisters in the Test Department"—his eyes went back again to Ashley— "actual maladministration on the part of the plant's responsible top executive might be involved. Actually we did find it very hard to dig out the facts, particularly since Leonard Tracy was severely burned in an accident shortly before Mr. Harris arrived here to take up his new duties. But Mr. Harris went on with his quiet undercover digging and eventually, quite recently in fact, made at least one important discovery: that certain chemical analyses had been altered by a member of the chemical staff. I refer, of course, to the late Walter Keene."

Quentin Harris spoke quietly from the rear of the group. "When I found out about Keene I was so angry I made some remark to Mr. Flint about Keene's deserving to be killed. It was ironic, therefore, to find that after Keene's death I myself was suspected as the murderer."

"Keene was not fired," the General continued. "In fact, we took particular care not to alarm him in any way. We knew Keene was nothing more than a pawn in the game. Falsifying the chemical analyses was the easiest part. We knew that someone with a thorough knowledge of the steel business must be involved, someone with opportunity and enough experience to fool qualified outside inspectors. So Keene was kept on the job in the hope that we might be able to trace the higher-up through that source."

He paused shortly and Ashley seized the opportunity to protest again. "I find it very hard to believe there has been crookedness in my department. I presume you have some definite—"

The General's look cut him short. "Plenty of proof," he said savagely. "But it wasn't until last night we knew Benjamin Gaylord was the man we were after."

Gaylord was plucking nervously at his colorless mustache. "You've made a terrible mistake. I haven't..."

"No use trying to bluff," the General said. "Your friends Sisco and Kosleck are both in the hands of the police. They've already spoken their piece, Gaylord, to save their own necks on the murder rap."

"Do I understand that Benjamin Gaylord is the person who committed these terrible crimes?" It was Ashley again. The tall, stoop-shouldered

Engineer of Tests wore a new look of righteous indignation on his scholarly face.

This time the General ignored the man completely. "Gaylord has been getting away with murder for a long time," he said. He swung suddenly to Glenn Cannon. "Back even in the days when you, Cannon, were Ironton's Chief Inspector. He was helped when necessary, by Keene on the chemical end."

Frantically Gaylord cried, "I didn't kill Walter! I didn't! You've got to believe me."

The skin was stretched even tighter than usual across the man's high cheekbones. His receding chin quivered weakly.

The General gave him a look of contempt. "I wouldn't believe you under oath, Gaylord. But it so happens you are not the *only* bad egg connected with the local Test Department." His eyes traveled back to Glenn Cannon. "You were framed, of course," he said, "you and young Locke as well."

For once Glenn Cannons face expressed emotion. Ray saw the man's look of relief as he glanced quickly at Jackie North.

Ray's eyes followed Cannon's. He noted that the girl's pretty face was white beneath her make-up.

"Miss North," the General continued, "allow me to congratulate you! You and Cannon together have done a beautiful job of confusing the issue. You managed to be virtually on the spot at the time both murders were committed. Only the fact that you were hiding in the dark rear office kept you from seeing the murderer carry Keene's body upstairs after his skull had been shattered. Again, you actually stumbled across Tracy's body only a matter of minutes after he had been decapitated. Only an overworked guardian angel has kept the two of you from really serious trouble."

Color was flooding back into Jackie's pale cheeks. "We thought the old records might show…"

"It's too late for explanations," the General said severely. "You managed throughout to make additional trouble for the police and for me. In addition you caused acute embarrassment to your boss, Mr. Harris."

"I denied having asked you to look over the records for me," Harris put in, "because Mr. Flint was not yet ready to expose my connection with his investigation. You almost upset the whole apple cart, Miss North."

"I'm dreadfully sorry," the girl said. "I suppose I should have told you the truth immediately."

"Yes," the General agreed coldly. "It would have simplified matters for us all. However, Mr. Harris himself removed the records in question night before last. Documentary evidence, proving that those axle test figures were altered, is now safely under lock and key, although in view of more recent developments, such records will not be needed."

Abruptly his finger shot out, pointing accusingly to Bixler. "You," he said, "are a murderer! You made one proven attempt—quite possibly two or more additional attempts—against young Locke. You richly deserve the hangman or the electric chair, for even though you were unsuccessful, your intentions were murderous. It's nothing more than dumb luck for you that you will not get either."

Bixler protested hoarsely, "I didn't do nothin'. I was just keepin' an eye on the kid. Mr. Tracy thought..."

"You will be rewarded as you deserve, Bixler. The company has no further need for your services and I rather imagine you will find it difficult to obtain a connection with any other large industry in America. I promise you I shall do my best to see that such is the case.

"Now don't interrupt," he snapped fiercely, as Bixler started to speak again. "I know you did a good deal of ugly, secret work for the late unlamented Leonard Tracy. Tracy was a man who lived by the sword. It is quite fitting that, in accordance with the Biblical prophecy, he should have perished by the sword."

Ulysses Flint tilted his head, his eyes fastening on the joists and beams above the tall test machine, as if he were studying the sooty cobwebs which had accumulated there.

"I want all you people to remember," he said, "that management is not gifted with omnipotence. The men at the head of the company's affairs make judgments based upon past records and the information at hand. No man's judgment is better than his information. Therefore, the management of American-Consolidated Steel had no reason to suspect that Leonard Tracy was a criminal. Yet he was—almost as great a criminal, as the one actually guilty of these murders."

Ray Locke's mind was whirling in hopeless confusion. To him, the General's explanations had thus far only succeeded in clouding the picture. A substantial number of possible suspects appeared to have been eliminated but there was still no indication of the actual killer's identity.

Jackie North and Glenn Cannon were both definitely out, according to Ulysses Flint. So were the smaller fry, the workmen, Sisco and Kosleck, and the dangerous company cop, Bixler.

Had the General meant to count out Gaylord as well? On this point Flint had been ambiguous. He had made no definite statement, but it was Ray's impression that Flint did not consider Gaylord to be the murderer.

"Leonard Tracy," the General was continuing, "was a great opportunist. To the public, the wreck of *The Prairie Comet* was a horrible tragedy. To the officials of American-Consolidated Steel it was not only a tragedy but a headache. But to Leonard Tracy the catastrophe came as the opportunity of a lifetime for the making of an enormous personal fortune. It was Tracy, therefore, who planted among Cannon's papers the forged letter which convicted both Cannon and Locke and sent them to the penitentiary!"

The General looked down from the ceiling then, and at Ray. "You labored for some time, Locke, under the delusion that Tracy was your friend. But before he died, I believe you had satisfied yourself of the reverse. Undoubtedly, Tracy gave you a job at Ironton for the sole purpose of making sure, with Bixler's help, that you would die inside this plant."

Ray's confusion was greater than ever. "But why?" he demanded. "What earthly reason did Tracy have for wanting to kill me?"

"That's what bothered me, too, for quite a time," the General admitted. "I've finally pieced the story together, with what I believe to be a fair degree of accuracy, from certain confidential sources of information open to my people in New York—bank sources. They revealed records of certain frenzied financing undertaken by Tracy; financial transactions of the late Belden Locke, before his tragic death in the wreck of the streamliner.

"You see, Ray"—it was the first time Flint had called Ray by his first name and Ray wondered at the sudden warmth of the big man's tone—"you see, your father had been working for some time before his death upon a new and superior process for the fixation of atmospheric nitrogen, a process which tied in closely with the steel industry. In fact it would enable the steel industry to recapture the importance of its former position as the leading producer of manufactured nitrogen, lost when byproduct coke-ovens came into competition with the Haber method of atmospheric fixation.

"It appears that Belden Locke, having successfully developed his new process in the laboratory, went to his friend Leonard Tracy with the suggestion that it be developed for commercial use through further experimentation at the Ironton Works. There were the inevitable 'bugs' to be overcome, problems of large scale production to be determined and solved. In consideration of his help and the privilege of utilizing Ironton's facilities, Tracy was to get a small percentage of the total royalties, when, as and if the new process came into widespread use in the steel industry. Did your father, Ray, ever mention any of this to you?"

Ray said, "He must have been working on it that year I was with Transcontinental. I was traveling almost constantly, ten nights out of eleven on a sleeper. He never once uttered the word 'nitrogen' in my presence."

The General nodded with satisfaction. "Just so. Belden Locke said nothing, even to his son. Leonard Tracy kept his mouth shut, too. Tracy should have consulted New York before making any such agreement involving use of the company's equipment, but he saw a chance for a huge personal profit. I am informed by New York that if this process comes into general usage in the steel industry, royalties might easily run to ten or twelve million a year. You see, then, it was no peanut stand affair. Even a man of stronger moral fiber than Leonard Tracy might have been tempted. Tracy risked his important and lucrative position against the probability of great wealth. Then came the wreck of the Transcontinental flyer. That wreck brought death to Belden Locke and to Tracy the chance of appropriating the entire process for himself."

A glimmer of light was beginning to clarify Ray's understanding. The hidden reason for Leonard Tracy's enmity was now revealed, and also the reason Belden Locke's entire resources had been drained away so inexplicably. What, Ray wondered, would be the final disposition of his father's process?

"Two obstacles confronted Tracy," Ulysses Flint was saying. "Most immediate was his fear that Belden Locke's son might stumble across the secret process among his father's effects. It was, therefore, providential for Tracy that the axle which caused the wreck had been manufactured here at the Ironton Works and from defective steel. The fact that Raymond Locke had been the inspector who accepted the steel for the railroad was one of those tremendous trifles which always have and always will determine the future course of events. Tracy was quick to seize upon this coincidence as his means for insuring against possibility of interference. He framed you, Ray, by planting a forged letter among Glenn Cannon's papers!"

"What about me?" Cannon asked.

"You," Ulysses Flint declared, "were simply a sacrificial victim upon the altar of Leonard Tracy's ambition. As a small part of his own plan, Tracy quite deliberately and cold-bloodedly wrecked your career."

A strangled sound came from deep in Cannon's throat. "If I'd known that I would really have been glad to kill him."

The General paid no further attention to Cannon, but went on with his story. "The other obstacle which confronted Tracy was less formidable. Full details of the process had not been furnished by Belden Locke. And Tracy was no scientist himself. He knew he would need expert technical assistance. But that offered no great difficulty since he had available at Ironton a full staff of technical experts. He entered into an agreement of his own with one of these technicians. They would go full steam ahead to work out the entire process, just as Belden Locke had intended to do. A small cut of the profits would go, this time, to the technician. Since the new process involved utilization of products of combustion from the open hearth and blast furnaces, an experimental laboratory was rigged under one of the furnaces in the Open Hearth. So far as other plant employees were concerned, this scientific workshop was kept strictly under wraps.

"Up to this time," the General went on, "everything had worked out smoothly for Tracy. But now things began to go sour. During preliminary tests of the apparatus, Tracy managed to get himself severely burned by the flame from the open hearth checker-work. He was in the hospital for several months. But he instructed his technical collaborator to go ahead with the research."

The big man swung suddenly to Benjamin Gaylord. "Incidentally, Gaylord, this type of scientific research would be far beyond your depth. Thus, when I began to understand the real motivations behind the crimes at Ironton, you were automatically eliminated from my list of possible suspects. Your dishonest activities have been on a petty scale only. You're only a small time chiseler and it's undoubtedly true that Leonard Tracy never had the slightest knowledge of your crookedness."

Benjamin Gaylord opened his mouth as if to speak. The General waited pointedly, a look of loathing for the man upon his face. Gaylord closed his mouth again without uttering a word.

"When Tracy came back from the hospital," Flint resumed, "the research was well advanced. Complete success was imminent. But by that time another obstacle had arisen in the path of the collaborators. It always happens when one embarks on a career of crime. Walter Keene, never averse to turning a dishonest dollar, as his activities in respect to the falsified tests have proven, had in some manner learned of the nitrogen research at the open hearth checker-work. Perhaps he demanded to be cut in on the proceeds. Exactly what happened then behind the scenes doesn't matter. The important climax came when Keene, finding that certain papers pertaining to the research were kept in a locked metal box, attempted forcibly to appropriate the box. Tracy's scientific collaborator was then obliged to make a sudden decision. That decision resulted in Keene's death.

"With the first murder quickly and successfully accomplished, the murderer had another inspiration—the same inspiration which occurred to Tracy after the train wreck. Why not squeeze Tracy out and appropriate the entire process? You see, greed has been the whole motivating influence in this affair from the very start, nothing but ordinary, ugly, sordid greed.

"Tracy knew nothing of the scientific details. His collaborator refused to give him the requested information. They must have had several angry altercations. Finally, to settle the matter beyond further doubt, the collaborator eliminated Tracy by decapitation with the alligator shears. The pattern of Eternal Justice is visible when we consider that Tracy, who initiated the whole series of crimes, ended as its final victim."

The General stopped talking. His black, inscrutable eyes moved slowly over all the faces before him. "Now," he said, "that I've made the background and motivation of these crimes clear to you all, I know you are anxious to know the identity of the killer."

He turned to Clara Dunne. "Miss Dunne, you told me not long ago that you thought my chances of finding the murderer among twenty thousand Ironton employees were nil. But the fact is, the killer left clues which definitely established his identity, even among so large a group— clues which definitely, inevitably stamped his guilt!"

Flints voice boomed accusingly. "You see, Miss Dunne, Mr. Ashley, who unquestionably has the necessary scientific attainment for pursuing the research on Locke's process for fixation of nitrogen, had an alibi for the time when Walter Keene was murdered. Or, I should say, he told us he had an alibi. Subsequent check of his time card seemed to bear out his statement. But further investigation on the part of Lieutenant Lambert and the homicide detail has shown conclusively that Christopher Ashley was actually inside the Ironton Works at two-thirty on the night of Keene's death."

SEVENTEEN

In the sudden breathless silence the mewing of the newborn kittens in the container behind the test machine rose plaintively. The eyes of everyone had shifted to Christopher Ashley.

The man's whole appearance seemed to have undergone a subtle change. His small, pointed beard no longer created an illusion of absent-minded scholarship. Instead, together with the shadows which the overhead light traced on Ashley's cheeks, it gave him a cruel, ruthless look, like the paintings of cold-blooded Spanish conquistadores from a bygone century.

Ashley's eyes, too, had lost their scholarly abstraction. They were arrogant now, hard. Yet deep below the surface they held a light of defiance as well—defiance and fear.

"It's a lie!" he said and his words were chill and precise. "I don't care who you are, Flint, it's a lie! You can't prove I was in the plant that night."

"Oh, but you're so wrong!" The General's voice was almost purring. "So wrong! You see, Ashley, we have a witness who actually saw you around the splice bar mill that night, and who is prepared to swear to it."

"Then your witness is a liar, too!"

"We'll produce two witnesses, or should I say one witness and one accomplice. The girl will testify, too, Ashley!"

Ashley was visibly shaken. "The girl! Well..." He collapsed quickly. "I did actually go to the splice bar mill, but—"

"Why didn't you tell us instead of lying?"

"I thought..."

"You wear a cloak of respectability, almost of righteousness," Flint interrupted. "Holier-than-thou and all that sort of stuff. But withal you're really a sanctimonious old fraud, Ashley. You didn't tell us you were in the plant because you wanted no one to suspect your extracurricular activities. Isn't that the fact?"

Ashley moistened his lips. He looked suddenly haggard. "It's true," he admitted. "But I know nothing of the murders. I swear I know nothing."

"I didn't say you did," the General retorted unexpectedly. "But I wanted to give you a bad fright. You deserved it, for the way you've been acting. Actually, you've been sowing a few wild oats. Right?"

Ashley nodded silently, biting his lips. His face was brick red.

"The boss," Ulysses Flint explained to Clara Dunne, "has been amusing himself with one of the girl chemists from your laboratory. He took her, that night, to the empty offices above the splice bar mill."

To Ashley again, he said, "New York isn't going to like it one bit. This company is in the business of making steel. It's not a missionary society. But moral turpitude, particularly among supervisory personnel, is something the management in New York despises." The General swung around again to Clara Dunne.

"And so we have eliminated everyone," he said. *"Except you!* But we really didn't need to follow the process of elimination. Because, as I remarked before, you left your individual stamp quite plainly on each victim." Ray was unaware that his mouth had dropped open. He stared in almost comic amazement, his eyes traveling from the General to the calm, emotionless face of Clara Dunne.

Even now, although Ulysses Flint had disposed of each possible murderer and named Clara as guilty, Ray could not believe it. Nor could he imagine how U. G. Flint had identified the red bruise on his head as the trademark of the stocky Chief Chemist.

The big man was bending now, pointing to the circular mark in the middle of his bald spot. "This, Miss Dunne, is what gives you away, even without further evidence. A similar mark was found on the head of each murdered man. Your method was remarkably simple, Miss Dunne— simple and efficient."

That would be like Clara, Ray was thinking. Anything she did would be done simply and efficiently, even murder.

"Your murder method must have come to you on the spur of the moment," the General went on, "probably at the time you found it necessary to do away with your troublesome assistant, Keene. Keene had been growing increasingly inquisitive about your work on the nitrogen research. He even tried, himself, to find the key to the Locke, as he called it, meaning, of course, the Locke Process. He knew you were working with the products of combustion from the open hearth furnace. He also managed to divine an additional application from the gases of the blast furnace. How near he came to learning something definite we will never know. But he must have worried you plenty. When he appropriated your brass box with the Chinese puzzle lock, in which you had temporarily placed certain recent data, you knew something must be done. You found him in the forge shop where he had broken open the box under a steam hammer. Action was imperative. So you removed your shoe, struck him on the head with the heel. Then, while he was still unconscious, you placed his head under the hammer and cracked his skull."

Clara Dunne had not lost her composure. In fact, she hadn't even changed color at the accusation.

"Ridiculous!" she said coolly. "Ridiculous on the face of it. How would I know how to run one of those big steam hammers?"

The General said, "Aha! That's a good point. We checked it very carefully, Lieutenant Lambert and I. We remembered what you told us about how you used to play around your father's metal-working plant when you were a small girl. That plant was actually a small forge shop, a *hammer* shop. We found out all about it, how you learned at that time to operate a steam hammer as well as a skilled hammer-man."

Clara stared at the General. Her eyes seemed bigger than usual, but except for that she was seemingly unmoved.

"The fact that it would look like the sort of crime no woman would commit was why you killed Keene that peculiar way!" the General went on remorselessly. "And it was the reason you took a chance on carrying his dead body back to the laboratory. That required strength. But you're a husky woman, Miss Dunne. You'd be perfectly capable of lifting a little runt like Keene.

"The killing of Walter Keene was a matter of impulse. But your other crimes were executed with precise premeditation. Tracy came twice to the laboratory to see you the day of his death. Probably he was putting increasing pressure on you to obtain the data on your nitrogen tests. So you decided to kill him.

"At the same time, you discovered—maybe Tracy told you about it— that young Locke had found your research laboratory beneath the open hearth furnace. Locke was dangerous for several reasons. You knew his habit of napping in odd places. So you followed him to the plate mill and managed to spill acid on the crane ropes as they dragged on the ground, hoping a falling plate would eliminate Locke. You were nearly success-ful. But your presence in the plate mill was noted by the crane operator who mentioned it to me when I questioned him later. Also the fact that acid had been used was, I found, a most revealing circumstance."

Ray was noting the courteous manner in which Ulysses Flint still addressed Clara, even while he accused her of unbelievable crimes. Evidently, the big man's deference toward women was something very deeply instilled.

"You were unsuccessful in your attempt on Locke," the General re-sumed. "But you got Tracy satisfactorily, Miss Dunne. You followed him from the Test Department building, struck him with your spike-heel, then lifted his head between the shear blades. That, again, was a crime which would not normally he associated with a woman.

"After concluding two killings without detection, I'm rather afraid you approached the state known as 'kill-crazy.' One life or a dozen, what difference did it make so long as you could safeguard the secret of the Locke Process, and insure that it would become the *Dunne* Process? You made another abortive murder attempt, this time against a meddlesome person by the name of U. G. Flint." His blunt fingers rubbed the bruise on his head tenderly. "Fortunately, I was saved from suffocation or roasting by my young friend Locke."

He stopped and Clara Dunne found her voice.

"The case you've built against me sounds quite convincing," she said icily. "Luckily for me, it is entirely supposition without a shred of actual proof. Even if the mark of my heel plate should coincide with the bruise on your head, Mr. Flint, I believe any jury would take into consideration the fact that someone besides myself might have used the shoe."

"You're quite right," the General admitted. "My evidence is strong: your ability to operate a steam hammer; your use of acid upon the wire ropes of the plate mill crane; the timing of your movements throughout; and most conclusive, the marks of your heel plate. First class evidence, but circumstantial—all of it. It would be exceedingly difficult to bang a pretty woman on circumstantial evidence alone. Furthermore, I hate circumstantial evidence. It's always sloppy, and more than once it has hanged an innocent person. Therefore, I decided to catch you in the act of attempted murder, red-handed, as the expression goes. And that I have just done, Miss Dunne, with live bait in the person of young Locke."

"You still can't prove…"

"This morning," the General said, "I told you, quite casually, that Locke had phoned me and would be in the lab this evening. I also mentioned that he had hinted at something concerning a new nitrogen process. I said nothing definite but contrived to give you the idea that after Locke had once seen me, you would be exposed. Your guilty mind, I knew, would read between the lines and you would make another effort to kill."

His eyes roamed the circle of tense faces. "The rest of you were requested to be in Tracy's office at the Administration Building at eight. I wished to leave the coast absolutely clear for Miss Dunne. But she gave me, again, a demonstration of her intelligence and cunning. Evidently she sensed the trap, and, investigating, discovered that all except herself were to be elsewhere. So she called the plant switchboard, pretending to be speaking at my request, and asked that you all be notified that the place of meeting had been changed to the chemical laboratory. Thus she expected to have all the suspects on the scene of her latest killing…the killing of Raymond Locke.

"In only one respect did she nearly slip. She failed to include Bixler among my invited guests. And, accordingly, having waited until everyone else was assembled here tonight, she came down to make her attempt. Instead she ran into Bixler at the foot of the stairs. Had Bixler been a single minute later he might have blundered into her in the very act of striking down young Locke.

"As it happened, she did meet him and therefore went back upstairs for a moment. Then she returned to stage her third murder, which Lieutenant Lambert and I have recorded on infra-red movie film through the Judas holes we bored in the wall of Ashley's office. That film, Miss Dunne, will provide proof that cannot fail to stand up against the most prejudiced jury."

Clara Dunne was speechless. But the way she kept her poise, even when she realized that she was hopelessly trapped, was truly remarkable.

Lieutenant Lambert stepped forward. "Clara Dunne," he said, repeating the formula ritual, "you are under arrest for the murder of Walter Keene and Leonard Tracy. I have to warn you that anything you say may be used against you."

"I have nothing to say," Clara told him stonily.

Ray said, "I have!" He fingered the swelling lump at the back of his head. "I was live bait, was I? Well, suppose I'd been shot? Or stabbed! It was rather a long chance, wasn't it, to take with a man's life?"

The General grinned. "I thought you might feel that way, Ray. That's the reason I didn't tell you the whole plan. I knew, of course, that Miss Dunne would follow her usual pattern; first the slipper, stunning the victim, then machinery of some sort to finish the job. It's been a case of 'heads, you lose,' from the very beginning. There was no reason for her to deviate in this case. So I took the precaution of learning how to control each machine in this laboratory and I was ready to step out instantly. Which I did."

"Lots of fun," Ray said bitterly, "being batted over the head and then nearly squeezed to death!"

"A sore head," Ulysses Flint observed cheerfully, "is a very small price to pay for what you have achieved, Ray. You're quite vindicated, of course, on every count—you and Cannon both. Incidentally, Cannon, I thought I specifically ordered *you* to keep away from Ironton."

It was Jackie North who answered. "I phoned him. After the message that I was to come here instead of to Mr. Tracy's office, I knew something was in the wind."

"My curiosity got the better of me. I just couldn't stay away," Cannon added.

"Fortunately you did no harm." The General turned again to Ray. "When the contents of Miss Dunne's safe deposit box are examined," he said, "as they will be in the due process of law, I feel quite certain there will be data there regarding your father's nitrogen fixation process. I also feel sure New York—the bank, you know—will be only too glad to help you get the process into general usage." The big man gave him a friendly grin. "You should find yourself an exceedingly wealthy young man."

Color touched the prison pallor of Ray Locke's cheeks. His eyes met those of Jackie North. "If I'm going to be rich," he said, "one of the most important things I'll need is a good secretary."

Jackie North smiled and lowered her eyes.

Ray reached for the dice in his vest pocket, rattled them in his loosely cupped hand.

"Bones don't lie, Bixler," he remarked with an air of triumph. "But it looks as if they meant a couple of other guys."

37333417R00089

Made in the USA
Middletown, DE
27 November 2016